A MAN CALLED "TEN"

Tenadore Brian was of Irish ancestry, one of the few soldiers on the frontier actually born there.

At sixteen, his family wiped out by an Indian raid, Brian had left the Plains country and gone off to sea. He joined the Foreign Legion, left it after seven years of tribal war for the Papal Zouaves. Nothing could hold him; soon he was off to China. Now he was back in the States, a lieutenant on the lonely frontier.

"Ten" had grown up with the Indians, hunted and played with them. Now he was on the other side and the future was written in flames.

UNDER THE SWEETWATER RIM
by LOUIS L'AMOUR

Bantam Books by Louis L'Amour
Ask your bookseller for the books you have missed

BRIONNE
THE BROKEN GUN
THE BURNING HILLS
THE CALIFORNIOS
CALLAGHEN
CATLOW
CHANCY
CONAGHER
DARK CANYON
THE DAYBREAKERS
DOWN THE LONG HILLS
THE EMPTY LAND
FALLON
THE FERGUSON RIFLE
THE FIRST FAST DRAW
FLINT
GALLOWAY
GUNS OF THE TIMBERLANDS
HANGING WOMAN CREEK
THE HIGH GRADERS
HIGH LONESOME
HOW THE WEST WAS WON
THE KEY-LOCK MAN
KID RODELO
KILLOE
KILRONE
KIOWA TRAIL
LANDO
THE LONELY MEN

THE MAN CALLED NOON
THE MAN FROM THE
  BROKEN HILLS
THE MAN FROM SKIBBEREEN
MATAGORDA
MOJAVE CROSSING
MUSTANG MAN
NORTH TO THE RAILS
OVER ON THE DRY SIDE
THE QUICK AND THE DEAD
RADIGAN
REILLY'S LUCK
RIDE THE DARK TRAIL
THE RIDER OF LOST CREEK
RIVERS WEST
SACKETT
THE SACKETT BRAND
SACKETT'S LAND
SHALAKO
SILVER CANYON
SITKA
THE SKY-LINERS
TAGGART
TREASURE MOUNTAIN
TUCKER
UNDER THE SWEETWATER RIM
WAR PARTY
WESTWARD THE TIDE
WHERE THE LONG GRASS BLOWS

Louis L'Amour
Under the Sweetwater Rim

BANTAM BOOKS
TORONTO · NEW YORK · LONDON

UNDER THE SWEETWATER RIM

A Bantam Book / May 1971

2nd printing	...... June 1971	7th printing	...... May 1973
3rd printing	.... August 1971	8th printing	... January 1974
4th printing	.. November 1971	9th printing	... October 1974
5th printing	..... March 1972	10th printing	...... July 1975
6th printing	..... August 1972	11th printing	. November 1975

12th printing ... February 1977

13th printing

ISBN 0-553-10901-4

Published simultaneously in the United States and Canada

Bantam Books are published by Bantam Books, Inc. Its trade-
mark, consisting of the words "Bantam Books" and the por-
trayal of a bantam, is registered in the United States Patent
Office and in other countries. Marca Registrada. Bantam
Books, Inc., 666 Fifth Avenue, New York, New York 10019.

TO GEORGE AND MARIAN . . .

UNDER THE SWEETWATER RIM

Chapter 1

They had ridden twenty miles since daylight, and at the end of their day had come upon disaster.

Two hundred feet below and half a mile away the wagon train lay scattered on the freshening green of the April grass. Death had come quickly and struck hard, leaving the burned wagons, the stripped and naked bodies, unnaturally white beneath the sun.

The man in the ill-smelling buckskins brought his mount alongside Major Devereaux. "There was fifteen wagons. You can even count 'em from here. The way they're strung out they must've been hit without warnin'. Looks like a few tried to pull out of line, like to form a circle, but they hadn't no time."

"One wagon missing, then."

Plunkett's head swung sharply around. "Now that ain't likely, Major, ain't likely a-tall. No Injun is goin' to haul a wagon away, an' nothin' that big is goin' to slip off unseen. Like you can see, they was caught in the open."

Major Devereaux did not explain. They were drawing nearer as they talked and he was studying the charred wagons, forcing himself to consider only the problems his duty imposed. If Mary was down there he would know soon enough, and the decision he must make would affect the lives of the entire command.

1

Aside from Lieutenant Tom Cahill, Sergeant Gogarty, and Plunkett, sixty men made up the patrol, forty-two of them raw recruits. They were two hundred miles west of Fort Laramie, carrying rations for the return and for two days extra, in case of emergencies.

Throughout the severe winter of 1863 and 1864, the Cheyennes and Arapahoes had remained quiet, but there had been persistent rumors of Sioux agents in their lodges. Undoubtedly they would be riding the war trail with first grass.

Major Devereaux, with twenty-seven years of service, was aware that the lives of men are dictated to an extent far greater than most men wish to admit, by events beyond their control. Man rides the ocean of history and does what he can to weather its storms.

He was aware that if his patrol became engaged this far from Fort Laramie it could expect no assistance. His orders were to avoid trouble if possible, make a display of strength, and hope the sight of their uniforms would restrain any ambitious warriors.

Far away to the east, and months ago, a great victory had been won at Gettysburg, but it had brought no relief to the frontier. Only a few days before the command left the Fort, the commanding general had withdrawn every man who could be spared from the Indian frontier to meet a force of Confederate troops assembled south of the Arkansas River.

Plunkett was obviously correct. It would have been impossible for an army ambulance to escape during such an attack. If the wagon was missing, it must have left the train sometime *before* the attack, which made no sense at all. Why, in the heart of Indian country, with attack imminent, would one wagon abandon the comparative safety of the wagon train? And where could it have gone? Where could it have planned to go?

Lieutenant Tom Cahill remained silent, but when Plunkett had ridden away, he said, "The ambulance your daughter was in, sir, had wider tires than usual.

2

Sergeant Gogarty explained their advantage to me before the wagons left the Fort."

Wide tires sank less deeply into the prairie, and therefore the wagons pulled more easily, but few of the ambulances were so equipped. Cahill, Devereaux reminded himself, was an observant young man and he was not above learning from the enlisted men when opportunity offered. The ability to observe with intelligence and to learn from all who could teach were invaluable qualities.

Devereaux turned in his saddle. "Sergeant Gogarty, take a burial detail and attend to that situation. If there are means of identifying the bodies, please make a note in each case."

"Sir," Cahill persisted, "what I wish to point out is that no such tracks were in the wagon trails when we intercepted their route. If a wagon turned off it must have been that wagon, and it must have turned off more than a dozen miles back."

Major Mark Devereaux looked down at the charred remains and sat still. Was Mary down there? He was not brave enough to attempt to identify her body, for if he found her all hope would be gone, and without Mary he would be nothing. He would be merely an old man, nearing retirement, with nothing before him but gray years until death.

His years of military service had left him with little but experience, and with nothing to leave Mary if he was killed in line of duty, or died of those ills the flesh is heir to. His greatest wish was for her to marry well, and it was this that led to his objections to Lieutenant Tenadore Brian, and to her presence with this wagon train.

Like many others of the Indian-fighting army, Tenadore Brian was of Irish ancestry, and was one of the few soldiers who fought on the frontier who had also been born there.

At sixteen, his family wiped out by an Indian raid,

3

Brian had left the Plains country and gone off to sea. Two years later he had joined the Foreign Legion, and was engaged for seven years in war against the fierce desert tribes. There he won a battlefield commission and two decorations.

Leaving the Legion, he had joined the Papal Zouaves, on guard at the Vatican, but after a year he had gone to China, advancing after a few rapid campaigns to the rank of general. When he returned from China he had another medal and a sword-cut on his cheekbone. Back in the States he was commissioned a lieutenant and was shipped to the frontier.

Lieutenant Tenadore Brian was a tall, lean, wide-shouldered man of thirty, with a rakish, devil-may-care look to him, a look enhanced by the scar on his cheek. Without doubt there was no more admired officer on the frontier, and his men worshipped him. He was the best rifle and pistol shot in the command, and an excellent swordsman. It was rumored that he had left the Papal Zouaves after killing one of the "black" nobility in a duel.

Major Devereaux had discovered him to be a shrewd, intelligent officer who took no unnecessary risks, and one who possessed an amazing knowledge of military tactics and history. No man that he knew could take out a mounted patrol and bring both men and horses back in better condition than when they left, no man but Brian.

He knew Indians as well as did the civilian scouts. As a boy he had hunted and played with them, learning their customs and their language. In the Sahara region he had found the tactics of the desert tribesmen similar to those of the Indians.

Although admiring Ten Brian's skill as a soldier, Major Devereaux considered him a foot-loose, drifting ne'er-do-well, an unfit associate for his daughter, not to be thought of as a potential husband.

Obviously, Mary had other ideas. For the first time

4

she had become interested in an officer. She had danced with many, gone with a few to parties, but on the whole her manner had been reserved around army men, and Devereaux had been content. And then she had seen Ten Brian.

Suddenly Brian had applied to the commanding officer for a week's leave, and left the post at once. Scarcely had he gone when Belle Renick, the matronly but attractive wife of Captain John Renick, announced her intention of traveling to California for a visit. Devereaux seized the opportunity to send Mary to her aunt in San Francisco. He was determined to break the attachment, once and for all.

Devereaux had even tried to use his rank and influence to get Brian shifted to Washington, his argument being Brian's aptitude for languages.

Remembering the look Lt. Col. Collins had given him, Devereaux flushed. "Mark," Collins had said, "I would like to do something for you. Anything but that. You must realize that Lieutenant Brian is amazingly equipped for our work. I couldn't spare him." Then he added, "Give it some thought, Mark. Mary might do a lot worse. That young man could go far, just as far as he wishes, and Mary might be just the influence he needs."

Abruptly, Devereaux brought his thoughts back to the present situation.

It lacked an hour to sundown and the men needed rest. He gave the order, and they moved upstream and camped in the bottom of a valley two miles from the scene of the massacre.

Cahill, he realized suddenly, had not mentioned the tracks of the ambulance until Plunkett was no longer near them. Was that mere accident? Or did Cahill share his distrust of the man?

Devereaux considered what he knew of Plunkett. The present commandant had acquired the services of the scout along with the command, and he had proved

5

valuable. A skilled tracker, he spoke several of the Indian languages, and he knew the country. Prior to service with the army he had been employed by the stage company in the time of Jules Reni. He was a tough, sour-smelling old man with no friends among army personnel. As a civilian employee, he came and went as he chose.

Plunkett had been absent from the Fort when the sixteenth wagon joined the train, and when they left the post. Devereaux and his patrol, with Plunkett as scout, had not come upon the trail of the wagons until shortly before reaching the scene of the massacre.

Realizing he disliked the man, Devereaux reserved judgment, but Gogarty was almost as good a tracker, and it might be just as well if the Sergeant was given the chance to do a little scouting.

Devereaux hesitated over calling on Turpenning, and then decided against it. The man from the Smokies was a hunter and a trapper, and the Major knew that Gogarty considered him the best tracker he had ever seen, even including Indians.

Devereaux was seated by the fire when Gogarty reported. "All identified but two, sir. We know who they were, but the way they were cut up it's hard to tell which is which."

"Did you find Mrs. Renick?"

"No, sir. Nor Corporal West nor Schwartz, nor any of them with the ambulance, sir."

"Thank you, Sergeant." He hesitated to ask Gogarty to scout the country before dark. He himself was bone-tired, and he knew the Sergeant must be also.

"Sir?"

"Yes?"

"I was about to ask, sir, that I be allowed to do some looking around. It won't be dark for half an hour yet."

"Thank you, Sergeant. I know you are tired, and I hesitated to ask you. But there's one thing. Whatever

6

you find, you are not to mention it to anyone but me. In the event that I should be unable to receive your communications, you are to give them to Lieutenant Cahill."

After Gogarty had gone, Major Devereaux tried to exclude all thought of Mary from his mind. He knew he must be dispassionate; he must examine the problem coldly in the light of the military situation and the risk to his command.

He was still thinking about it when Cahill returned. "If you will forgive me, sir. I know you are worried, and I thought ... well, sir, Lieutenant Brian might have returned."

For a moment Devereaux's mind refused to accept the idea, suggesting an element he had not considered. The relevancy escaped him. "What do you mean?" he asked. "I fail to see the connection."

Cahill flushed. "I am sorry, sir. It is none of my affair, but . . . well, Lieutenant Brian seemed very interested in Miss Devereaux, and she in him. I thought . . . well, they might have reached an understanding."

"I believe you are mistaken, Lieutenant. In any event, Lieutenant Brian left the post several days ago."

"No, sir."

"What?"

"One of the . . ." Cahill hesitated. "I mean, sir, Ten Brian did not go east. He was seen in Julesburg by one of the enlisted men."

Major Devereaux's lips tightened. Mary had deceived him. Yet even as he thought this, fairness cooled his anger. She had made no promises. She had simply agreed to go with Belle Renick.

But as he considered the idea his suspicions grew. Mary was like her mother in that she rarely opposed him but, like her mother, when she was determined she had not hesitated to act on her own. A faint smile softened his hard mouth at the thought of his dead wife. Susan had seemed so submissive that few realized the clearness of her thinking, or how determined she could be when convinced she was right.

Even as the memory of his wife softened his feeling toward Mary, his anger hardened toward Ten Brian. The man was an adventurer, shifting from place to place and from girl to girl as the whim took him. It was his influence that had brought this situation about, and if Cahill was right there was no telling where they were or what might happen to them.

But the thought uppermost in his mind was that they were not dead back there with the others, and they still had a chance for survival.

"Thank you, Lieutenant," he said. "Now if you will check the bivouac area. I shall also want a report on the placing of the guards. You understand, Lieutenant, the Indians who attacked that wagon train were armed, and they now have whatever guns and ammunition were captured. They must be considered extremely dangerous."

"Yes, sir. I understand, sir."

It was not until he started to remove his boots that Major Devereaux realized how tired he was. *"Mark,"* he said to himself, *"you're not getting any younger."*

Turpenning appeared from the shadows. "Coffee, suh?"

"Thank you, Turpenning."

The soldier lingered, and Devereaux waited, knowing the man had something on his mind. Most of the enlisted men were afraid of Devereaux, for he had the name of being a strict disciplinarian, but Turpenning had never seemed awed by that reputation.

"Was there something else, Turpenning?"

"Major, we all know Miss Mary was with those wagons, an' likewise we know we're travelin' on short rations, but the boys, suh, they elected me to tell you that if you're of a mind to search, they'll stretch rations, or go without grub. They'll stay with you as long as need be."

8

Devereaux was touched. Never in his military career had such an offer been made to him. He knew he was respected, but this he had not expected; yet he was rational enough to realize that it was mostly because of Mary herself. She was unfailingly gracious, always thoughtful and considerate of the feelings of the enlisted men.

"Thank them for me, Turpenning. I appreciate it, but the command must hold strictly to its orders."

Still the man did not leave. "Suh, we're just a-hopin' you won't cut it any finer for Miss Mary than for any other woman who might be out there. We're just a-hopin' you'll throw away the book an' let us go find her."

"That will be all, Turpenning."

"Yes, suh." The Tennessean saluted and turned away into the darkness.

Devereaux waited until the final report. Nine women, fourteen children, and twenty-one men, all dead, all mutilated.

When he settled into his blankets he was thinking of Mary. She was out there somewhere. He could not and would not believe her dead. Somehow, somewhere, her wagon had turned off, leaving the seeming security of the wagon train to travel alone. To where? For what?

He awoke in the chill of the pre-dawn darkness with a hand on his shoulder. "Sir? Can you come? There's something out there in the dark . . . something hurt."

Chapter 2

Harrison, the corporal of the guard, was not a man to be disturbed by shadows. Major Devereaux threw off his blankets and, shivering at the morning chill, reached for his boots. Nearby, Cahill was tugging on his.

It was still dark. The coals of the campfires were a dull red glow; a tiny flame flickered about one last twig in his own fire. Mark Devereaux followed Harrison through the camp in the direction of the trouble.

At the camp's edge they paused to listen. They heard a rustle of water, and a faint stirring in the brush across the stream. A whimpering sound came to them, the sound of an animal in pain.

Cahill drew his pistol. "Sir, I am going down there. That's an injured man."

Ignoring Harrison's whispered protest, Devereaux followed, though it was an irresponsible thing to risk both officers at one time, in such a place.

Under the trees it was even darker. When they could make out anything they could see a faint shine of light on brass buttons. At that moment there was a low moan, and the brush crackled as the wounded man tried to heave himself onward.

A gun flashed, and something struck with a thud into a tree near Devereaux.

10

Cahill and Devereaux fired at the same time, and a second bullet clipped a twig from a branch over Cahill's head. Someone rushed, then crashed in the brush and was still.

Cahill knelt beside the wounded man. "It's Gogarty, sir. He's bought it."

Devereaux dropped to his knee. "Wagon . . . west of here." The words were mumbled through bloody froth. "Three riders. One of them is Brian, sir."

Their eyes were accustomed to the darkness now, and they could see his skull was matted with blood, his uniform shirt stiff with it. How he had made it this far was one of those small miracles that are forever happening to tough men.

"What tribe, Sergeant? What kind of Indians?"

Gogarty tried to speak. "Don't trust . . . Plunkett is . . ." The dying man caught at Devereaux's sleeve. "No Indians! No . . ."

His voice faded out, and Devereaux spoke loudly, hoping to get his words through to him. "You're a good soldier, Gogarty. There are none better."

He felt the Sergeant's grip tighten momentarily on his arm. It might have been a twitch of dying muscles. The Major hoped it was a response to his words, for he knew what such words could mean to an old campaigner.

Harrison came up to them. "You hit something across the creek, sir. Turpenning has gone to look."

Cahill sat back on his heels. "The Sergeant is dead, sir," he said.

The sky was growing gray with faint light showing through the trees. Yes, Gogarty was dead. How many patrols they had ridden together. How much dust they had shared from Texas to Dakota, from Wyoming to Arizona.

The creek was a dozen feet wide and no more than six inches deep. Turpenning stood beside the man they had shot. A bullet had ripped through his chest and

11

smashed his spine, and another had torn through his stomach. He had lived only long enough to know that he was dying.

Turpenning turned the body over. It was Plunkett.

The man from the Smoky Mountains had found Plunkett's horse and led it near. "Somethin' here you should oughta see, suh." He indicated the saddlebags.

In one of the bags was a bandana handkerchief bulging with coins—some silver, some gold. There were also several rings, and two spare pistols.

"Loot," Cahill said, and with one finger he indicated a gold signet ring. "That belonged to Johnny Shaw."

Shaw had been a trooper of the 7th Iowa Cavalry, invalided to California after losing a leg in the service. He had been riding with the wagon train.

"Plunkett has been in touch with them, then." Devereaux was thinking aloud. "He has seen them since the massacre."

He thought back to attacks on other wagon trains. How many had Plunkett spotted for the renegades? For Plunkett was often off the post scouting for Indians, and he could easily have reported the movements of both troops and pioneers to whoever he worked with.

Gogarty had said they were not Indians, and until there was further evidence, Major Devereaux decided he would think of it that way. If they were renegade white men or Confederates sent west to stir up the Indians, the chances were they had been or would be coming into Julesburg. Men of that stripe would want to spend their money, and Julesburg was the closest place. They might be easier to trace than Indians.

"Request puhmission, suh?"

"What is it, Turpenning?"

"I'd like to take Plunkett's horse an' look about, suh."

"Go ahead. Report directly to me when you come in."

Plunkett and Gogarty had been buried, and breakfast was finished when Turpenning rode back into camp.

"Back-trailed Gogarty," he said, "an' found where Plunkett cut his sign. Plunkett rode up an' joined him, waited his chance, an' hit him over the head. I seen where Gogarty fell, seen the mark left by a bloody gun-butt. Seen where Plunkett wiped blood from his knife on the grass after stabbin' the Sarge.

"After Plunkett rode off, the Sarge, he dragged hisself maybe a hundred and fifty feet, grabbed a stirrup, pulled himself up an' got into the saddle. Plunkett, he must've heard him, come back an' took after him."

"You found wagon tracks?"

"I did, suh. Lieutenant Brian is with the wagon, suh. Seen the tracks of that big gray of his'n."

So . . . it was true, then.

"Suh, I got me a bad feelin' about that outfit. I mean those murderin' men. That's a bad bunch."

Devereaux was listening with only half his attention. He was thinking of Mary—of Mary and Tenadore Brian.

"Suh, they's maybe forty men in that outfit, well found and well mounted." He gestured toward the north. "They camped two, three days. Had grub to waste, because they wasted some. Stacked arms, an'—"

"*Stacked arms?*"

"Yes, suh."

A military command, then. Or a man who could enforce such discipline on rabble, and therefore a dangerous antagonist.

Forty seasoned men, and he himself had only sixty, most of them raw recruits who had never, so far as he knew, been under fire. And he could ill afford the loss of Sergeant Gogarty.

"What about those with the ambulance, Turpenning? Would you say they had knowledge of what happened to the wagon train?"

"I'd say so, suh. I don't know how that could be,

13

seein' when they left the train, but that Ten Brian, suh—beggin' your pardon, suh, *Lieutenant* Brian—he don't miss no tricks. He was holdin' that ambulance to low ground an' plenty of cover. I seen where he cut their trail . . . the one they made two, three days ago ridin' into the camp where they waited. He cut their trail an' he knows about them. He knows all about them."

The thought came to him then, came and was quickly dismissed as unworthy. But it returned, nagging for attention.

"Turpenning"—he spoke carefully—"could you identify the track of the leader's horse? I mean, could you tell which animal he rode?"

Turpenning hesitated only a moment, his eyes flickering to the Major's, then away. "No, suh. I surely couldn't."

Tom Cahill's head had come up, and Devereaux was conscious of his stare.

"You said the ambulance had gone west, didn't you? Not back toward the post?"

"West it was."

Mark Devereaux was silent, but his mind was piecing it together, fighting what common sense seemed to indicate. He was worried for fear his opinion was shaped by dislike. Was he allowing himself to be influenced by his conviction that a drifting man was an unreliable man?

"Lieutenant Brian," Devereaux said, "has overstayed his leave."

There was a moment of silence while they absorbed this fact and its ramifications. He had not only overstayed his leave, but the wagon in which Mary Devereaux and Belle Renick rode was being directed away from the post.

Brian had left the post before the wagons departed, and had been seen around Julesburg, a hangout for all the riffraff in the country around.

14

The ambulance was rolling westward. By keeping to low ground and under cover, it could not move as rapidly as its occupants might wish, and by a forced march it might be overtaken.

Major Devereaux mentally retraced the route back to Fort Laramie. By stretching a march here and there an extra day might be saved. A day saved and two days' extra rations meant three days in which to find his daughter and punish the renegades.

"Lieutenant Cahill, can you think of any reason other than the supposed understanding with my daughter why Lieutenant Brian should have joined the wagon train?"

"No, sir."

"Can you think of any reason why he should overstay his leave? Or why he should continue toward the west?"

"No, sir. Only—"

"Only what?"

"Fort Bridger, sir. He might be trying to reach Fort Bridger. It is closer than Laramie now, sir."

Of course. Major Devereaux was irritated that he had not considered that. It was the result of being so anxious to find Brian in the wrong. Nevertheless, a lot was left that needed explanation.

Why had Ten Brian gone to Julesburg when he should have gone to St. Louis?

"Corporal Harrison, you are acting sergeant. Cahill, if you will mount the command, we will move out. Turpenning, you will act as scout. Find the trail of the ambulance. I want to overtake it within twenty-four hours. When you find the tracks of the ambulance, the renegades, or anyone else, notify me at once. Is that clear?"

"Yes, suh. It is, suh."

As the command was formed, Devereaux reviewed the situation and found nothing good about it.

The grass was turning green, which meant there was

15

feed for the Indian horses. The Cheyennes and the Arapahoes would be riding the war trail. Collins would need every man at Fort Laramie, and every day, even every hour that he remained away from the post was a risk.

His orders allowed little room for deviation, but if he could recover the ambulance and return within the allotted time all would be well. As to the renegades, it was unlikely they would attack an army command, unlikely they would even show themselves, for their success in raiding depended on their not being known for what they were. Indians had been blamed, and they planned for the blame to continue to be placed on the Indians. Nevertheless, if opportunity offered . . .

A fight with the renegades, even if he won, would seriously cripple his patrol, a fact they could not conceal from the Indians. Roman Nose and Black Kettle could assemble two thousand warriors if need be, and there was much anger in the lodges.

The terrain as it opened before them was a succession of valleys divided by long ridges crested with pines, their slopes sometimes dotted with clumps of aspen. To the northwest, far beyond the ridges, loomed mountains heavily forested, still white with the winter's snow.

There was danger of ambush. From Plunkett, the renegades knew of Devereaux's force and its make-up. However, they were interested in loot and his command offered nothing but its horses, and horses might be obtained in easier ways.

Turpenning rode back. "Right through the trees there, suh. That's where the wagon trail lies."

"Turpenning," Major Devereaux said, "be careful. And if you come upon their camp, keep your eyes open for a man on watch. They will have pickets out, and I want a prisoner. If you find their camp, report to me at once."

16

To Major Mark Devereaux, the Army way was his life, but the frontier had a way of making light of the rule book, and he was wise enough to temper the rules with judgment. While his discipline was strict, his care for the health of his men and the condition of their horses and equipment was painstaking and thorough. Privations there would be, but most of them could be avoided by care in planning.

The same was true of military action. The ideal situation—and he had attained it twice—was where no battle need be fought. To put the opposing force in such a position that effective resistance was impossible —that was the ideal, and the two occasions when he had attained it were small actions, and his prisoners few in number.

As the column advanced he considered the situation. Ordinarily a renegade force would try to avoid battle with a military unit, but they might risk it. It was too bad, he reflected, that so much of a recruit's time was wasted on close-order drill, of use only for parade formations and in moving a command in an organized area. Such training was useless in combat; a recruit was taught everything except how to fight. The only way the army offered training in combat was by survival. If one survived in combat one was wiser and a better fighter next time.

When the command had been moving for two hours, Major Devereaux dismounted them under the edge of some trees for a short breather. He wanted both men and horses fresh if they came up with the enemy. He walked among them, checking the appearance of the men and their horses.

Cahill was waiting for him when he returned to the head of the column. "Sir, is it possible that you believe Lieutenant Brian to be in command of those renegades?"

"I have suggested no such thing, Lieutenant. However, there are questions to be answered. Brian was in Julesburg when he was believed to be elsewhere. He is now with the ambulance in which my daughter is riding. There is no explanation for his presence there. It alone evaded the massacre. One might believe that he had led the ambulance away deliberately before the massacre took place. That would imply prior knowledge.

"Furthermore, he is proceeding westward, he has overstayed his leave, and is making no effort to return to duty. That could imply intent to desert."

"But that's all supposition, sir," Cahill protested. "There could be other explanations."

"Of course. I shall be prepared to hear them. I believe you will admit that other explanations would be doubtful, to say the least."

He glanced at the sun. "Give them five minutes more, Lieutenant, then move them out."

"Ten Brian is my friend, sir. I cannot believe he would do anything dishonorable."

"Your loyalty does you credit. I hope he is worthy of it. Nonetheless, Lieutenant, if we come upon Lieutenant Brian he is to be put under arrest."

"Yes, sir. Is it necessary, sir?"

"It will be necessary. You will obey orders."

Cahill flushed. "Of course."

Devereaux watched Cahill walk away. Whatever else might be said of Brian, he thought, he inspired a unique kind of loyalty. There probably was not a man in the command who would not speak for him, or fight for him if necessary.

Mark Devereaux was not a man who took much for granted, not even with himself. Stern he might be, and a stickler for the letter of the law, but he was always questioning himself, and he wondered now how much of his suspicion was justified. Was he jealous?

Deliberately, he avoided thoughts of Mary. He must

be clear-headed, and be in a position to judge fairly. Doubt, fear, and emotion could cloud his judgment.

He led off at a fast walk, and after half a mile, to a trot. There was so little time.

Chapter 3

When the ambulance was hiddin within the mouth of the gully, and the horses returned from water, Ten Brian went out to do what he could to obliterate the tracks.

He had no illusions of escaping from the renegades or Indians. He knew his enemies too well to underrate their skill. What he did hope to do was keep from being discovered or captured until Major Devereaux's command came within marching distance.

At the same time he knew their chances were best to strike for Fort Bridger and safety. There was a limit beyond which Devereaux could not go, and the ambulance had nearly reached that limit now. So they must find a position from which they could observe the trail to the south and east, and if after a reasonable time they did not sight Devereaux's troops, they must make a run for it for Fort Bridger, roughly a hundred miles to the west.

Day had just come when Brian returned to the ambulance. Belle Renick was waiting for him. "Is it all right to make coffee? The men are worn out, Lieutenant."

"By all means. Ironhide will make you a fire. Nothing must go into the flames that will cause smoke, and the fire must be put out as soon as breakfast is over."

It was a risk, he knew, but coffee and a hot meal were a morale factor he dared not omit. Ironhide was a Cherokee, and he could be depended on as to the fire.

He started to turn away but her voice stopped him. "Lieutenant, I don't understand this at all. Why, if there was danger, did you take us away from the safety of the wagon train?"

"There was no safety there, Mrs. Renick. As I have said, you must trust me."

"But where are you taking us?"

Corporal West had come up with an armful of dry wood, and now he stood listening.

"I am trying to save your lives. The wagon train is gone . . . wiped out."

"You mean . . . all those people? They've been killed? Oh, no!"

"Mrs. Renick, I am as sure of it as if I had been there. I tried to warn them. I asked them to stop, to take up a strong position and wait for Major Devereaux's patrol. They wouldn't listen to me, so I used my rank to pull you people out of the train."

Her eyes searched his face. "I don't know what to think, Lieutenant, and I'm frightened."

"West, will you ask the other men to step over here? And Mrs. Renick, if you would ask Mary to come out."

"I *am* out."

Mary was standing at the back of the ambulance, a slender, strong girl with grave, serious eyes, watching him. He looked at her, and for a moment their eyes held, but he said nothing more, waiting for the men.

The air was crisp. Overhead the sky was cloudless blue. He could smell spring in the air, the earth coming alive.

Above on the left was a knoll. The gully was a short one, invisible until one was right upon it. A buffalo wallow had probably begun it, and water running from the knoll, had over the years cut the gully deeper with every rain.

Trees had grown up around it until in the hollow a wagon and horses could be concealed, allowing for a camp hidden from all eyes. The nearest water was a hundred yards off. There was nothing about this knoll to distinguish it from any other, and it seemed to offer no possible hiding place.

Schwartz was the teamster, a stocky, bull-headed German who had served in the old country. He was a good man, strong, unimaginative, dependable as the sunrise.

Ironhide, the Cherokee, born in eastern Oklahoma, was a veteran of six years in the cavalry. He was a tall man, slightly stooped; at twenty-three he looked thirty, and at sixty would probably still look thirty. He was a tough, tireless man, and a dead shot.

George Dorsey was a drifter, at various times a track-layer, a steamboat hand, a cattle drover. He had served two years in the 7th Iowa, and Brian suspected he had served elsewhere before that. Many of the Indian-fighting army had deserted at one time or another, then re-enlisted. They went over the hill, prospected or hunted buffalo for a time, got hungry, and enlisted again.

Dorsey had been on watch on top of the knoll.

"Did you see anything up there?" Brian asked.

"Nothing . . . not even an antelope."

Brian glanced at them briefly, then explained. "When I ordered you to leave the wagon train with me you may have believed me to be crazy, but I knew it was the only way I could save any of you.

"I had occasion to visit Julesburg, and as some of you may know, I grew up in this country. There was a man there I knew, and he passed the word to me that the wagon train would never reach South Pass. By the time I caught up with you the wagonmaster was sure you were out of danger. You will remember that I tried

22

to persuade him to fort up and wait, but he refused to consider it. I had no authority over him, but you were Army personnel."

Corporal West said, "I heard you tell Miss Devereaux the wagon train had been destroyed. How can you know that?"

"I cannot be sure, but yesterday we saw smoke rising from where the wagons should have been."

"They'd have been hard to take, Lieutenant. There were some good men in that outfit."

"My information was there would be forty or more seasoned fighters in the attacking party. Not Indians, but renegade white men who have been in this business for quite a while, possibly for years. The attackers could choose their own time, and catch the train in the open or when it was crossing a stream."

"You seem mighty sure, Lieutenant. Odd you should know all about this before ever it happened."

Ten Brian was cool. "I am almighty sure of one thing, Corporal West, that had I not come along you would now be lying among the dead. And let me say this. If anything happens to me you will be in command. I hope when you are you will recall what I am saying now. There is no more dangerous man alive than the one who leads that group, and we have not escaped them yet."

"You want to try for Fort Bridger?"

"Their headquarters is behind us, and they are now somewhere near. Their hunting ground is the country we have passed through, and if we wait they may turn back."

"Do they know about us?"

Brian shrugged. "If they do, they will come after us. They daren't let anybody escape. Also, they'll be wanting women."

Belle Renick interrupted. "The coffee is ready, and I've broiled some steaks."

After Dorsey had returned to the lookout on the

knoll, Brian turned again to West. "Corporal, I want you and Schwartz with the wagon and the women at all times. One of you must be awake always.

"Dorsey, Ironhide, and I will take turn about watching from the knoll."

When the others had moved off he sat again by the dying fire and filled his cup from the blackened pot.

"I am not sure I like this, Ten," Mary said.

"You are not alone—I like nothing about it."

"If we are off the trail like this, how will father ever find us?"

"He may be in so much trouble he won't have time to look. If you recall, your father has only a few veterans in that group. Most of the men have never heard a gun fired, as far as we know."

"Those men . . . they wouldn't attack the *army?*"

"They might. But only if they felt they had something to gain." He glanced at Belle. "Did the Captain give you a gun?"

"Yes."

"Keep it handy—you may need it. And neither of you must leave camp without telling Schwartz or West, and when you go, go together."

They sat in silence for a while, staring at the coals. "Ten, what are we going to do?" Mary asked presently.

"We'll stay right here for two or three days—it's an unlikely place to look. They won't look for us very long, I'm thinking, and after that we'll pull out for the west, keeping to high ground in the mountains."

The air was still, the sky was cloudless. Brian glanced at the knoll. There were no trees at the top, only a little brush and some dwarf cedar that grew from an outcropping of rock.

There was a small hollow up there, just large enough for three or four men. From the concealment it offered, anyone would have a three-hundred-and-sixty-degree field of fire, with no cover nearer than a hundred yards. However, at a point nearly that far away there rose

24

another hill, slightly higher than their own, and a good marksman on top of that hill could make this position untenable. This was the only drawback in their position here except for its lack of water. Two barrels on the sides of the ambulance, but rarely carried on such a vehicle, took care of that problem when the ambulance was near.

Ever since leaving the wagon train, Brian had taken precautions to erase as much of their trail as possible, but he knew that a skillful tracker could find them.

At noon he climbed the knoll and relieved Dorsey. "Get some sleep," he said. "You'll need it."

He settled down to studying the terrain. This would be a moonlight night, but rocks and trees have a way of looking different by night, and unless every one of them was memorized, a man might believe he was seeing things that he was not.

There was no use, he reflected, in telling them that the man at the head of the renegades was Reuben Kelsey. They had worries enough.

Kelsey had never won the reputation of some of the other border riders, like Quantrill or Bloody Bill Anderson, but he had been wise enough to shift his base of operations to the Emigrant Trail. The loot was better, there were Indians to take the blame, and there were no settlers to report their activities. Above all, Kelsey knew the country as few other men did.

Everybody knew about Reuben Kelsey, but the fact that he was operating this far west was not known. It had been reported that he had been seen in Kentucky, and even that he had been killed during a fight in Missouri. As for Ten Brian, he had made no secret of the fact that he had once known Kelsey, or that they had been friendly after a fashion.

Choctaw Benson had been the source of the information as to Kelsey's presence in Wyoming. Ten Brian as a boy had known Benson and liked the old mountain man, and he had come upon him again in a frontier saloon, after his own return to the frontier. He had bought him a drink, then staked him.

A few days later, as Brian was preparing for his trip to St. Louis, word had reached him that Benson wanted to see him. Brian hesitated because of his own plans, but Choctaw Benson had never made an urgent request before, so Brian had gone to Julesburg.

"Heard you was sweet on the Major's gal," Choctaw said, squinting his wise old eyes at him. "Well, you was always a good boy, so take care. Kelsey's seen her, and he's crazy after women. The way he uses them up they don't last long. There's a streak o' pizen in him. I seen a squaw he worked on one time, when he wanted to get shet o' her . . . well, I never seen an Apache who could have done it worse.

"Don't you take risk of him. He's handy with any kind o' weapon, an' he's more treacherous than a rattler. They give a body warnin', at least."

Kelsey's activities with women had been known along Suds Row, for gossip had a way of getting around. From Suds Row it had been repeated in the officers' quarters, and even Mary had probably heard the stories. Yet Kelsey could be ingratiating. Even as a boy he had winning qualities, as Brian remembered.

As Brian sat there on the knoll, someone came up the cut toward him. It was Mary.

She sat down beside him and looked through a space between the rocks at the wide plain. "Will they come that way?" she asked.

He shrugged, and indicated several other spaces that allowed a view over the surrounding area.

She locked her arms around her knees, and turning her head, regarded him calmly. "You knew of this place, Ten."

"Yes."

"I think you told me about it once. You hid here from the Indians . . . three days, wasn't it?"

"Yes," he said again.

26

"And over there somewhere"—she gestured toward the south—"your parents were killed."

"You have a good memory."

"There was another boy with you, a boy who lost his family in that attack."

"He wasn't with me here. We met the next day, over on the Sweetwater."

"You told me his name, too."

"Sometimes I talk too much."

"Ten, there's something you don't know that you should know. There's government money in our wagon."

He turned his head sharply, gripped by fear. Reuben Kelsey was sometimes lazy, and he might give up a chase if it looked too hard, and wait for an easier prey. After all, there were other women; but for women and money both, he wouldn't give up at all.

"Who knows this besides you?"

"Belle . . . and Corporal West. He's not guarding us, he's guarding the money."

"How much money?"

"Sixty thousand dollars . . . in *gold*."

Sixty thousand dollars! Reuben Kelsey must have known, tipped off by someone. No wonder he had attacked the wagon train.

It had twenty-odd men, some of them known fighters, and it would not be Kelsey's usual game; but he had attacked and he had wiped them out, men, women, and children, but he had found no gold, no army wagon or ambulance, no army personnel.

That could mean but one thing. Rueben Kelsey would not return to his hide-out. He would know that the ambulance carrying that gold was out here somewhere, and he would not give up until he had found it . . . and Mary.

Chapter 4

The sun was warm, pleasantly so. Nothing moved on the wide plain. In the west, on the horizon, loomed the Wind River Mountains.

"We can't outrun them," Brian was saying, "although if we left the ambulance . . ."

There really was very little choice. The ambulance was light and moved easily. The trail they had followed was wide and had been traveled by the wagons of the Forty-Niners, as well as pioneers bound for Oregon, so that presented no problem. The trouble was that hiding an ambulance is rarely easy; hiding its tracks even harder.

"I must find out where they are," he went on. "I know they are within a few miles."

"My father is on patrol," Mary said, "but I don't know how far he was to come. Anyway, he could not find us, hidden like this."

"Turpenning could." Brian paused. "I doubt if your father would come so far as this. He might, given the right conditions, but they are so short of men that Collins would not want him away from the post for too long a time. No, we must not think of what he might do. What is done we must do ourselves. We must make our plans with care, and when we move it must be with speed and discretion."

"Shouldn't we be moving now?"

"We'll wait. As long as we do not move, we will leave no tracks, and we'll raise no dust."

The afternoon drifted slowly by. The soldiers, glad of the rest, slept, loafed in the shade, and watched the shadows pass. Only Corporal West seemed thoughtful and morose, glancing from time to time at the knoll where Brian was on watch.

He had admired Ten Brian, but now he felt he was an antagonist, though with no reason he could name. Corporal West had been in command of the ambulance and that command had been usurped; with the command went the responsibility, of which West was glad to be free.

But he was suspicious of Brian. He had ridden up suddenly from nowhere, demanding the ambulance turn off and abandon the train.

At first West had believed in the fear that Brian communicated, but he no longer felt so sure. After all, sixty thousand dollars was a lot of money, and it was not as if the Lieutenant was a career soldier. He had left armies before this and could again. West had known men to desert for a lot less, and said so to Dorsey.

"Sixty *thousand?* Who's got that kind of money?"

West was annoyed with himself. He had been expressly warned to say nothing about the money, yet it had come out. In any event, it was too late now.

"What do you think we're guarding? The women?"

Dorsey whistled softly, glancing awe-struck at the ambulance.

When the Cherokee came up the cut with the last rays of the sun, Ten Brian sat beside him indicating the various approaches. Like many Cherokees, he was a man of education, reading easily not only in his own language as devised by Sequoyah, but in English.

"Is it true, Lieutenant, that you know Reuben Kelsey?"

29

"I knew him as a boy, and then a few years later, but I haven't seen him since we were sixteen."

"You were friends?"

"We worked together, fought side by side, escaped from the Cheyennes together, but it is not a friendship I would trust where money or women are concerned."

"I see."

"Will he find us?"

"I think so. How soon, is the question. If they lose our trail down there they may go west, or turn back toward Laramie, looking for us. Then we must move."

"You know about the money?"

Brian, startled, glanced at him.

Ironhide smiled. "Oh, yes! We know about it, Lieutenant. Or at least I did. I helped load it."

Brian was displeased. Did everybody know about that damned gold? Ironhide he could trust. Actually, he was the only soldier of the lot whom he knew. The others he had seen about the post, but Ironhide had actually served with him on a scout down toward Big Timbers.

Schwartz seemed a good solid man. Dorsey? There was a question in his mind about Dorsey. He would not want his honesty to be stretched too far, but Dorsey was a good soldier, and a good rifleman.

At daybreak, after Dorsey had relieved Ironhide, the Cherokee and Ten Brian took the horses to water. There was plenty of water in the barrels but the animals required a good deal and he did not want to deplete his supply too much. There were nine horses— the four hitched to the ambulance, and the mounts for each of them except Schwartz and Belle.

"There's grass enough for another day," West said. "What are we to do?"

Tenadore Brian stared into the coals of the fire. Belle was trying to heat the coffee with as little fire as possible. He waited just a moment, searching his mind for any ideas that might offer alternatives. Then he said,

30

"We're leaving the ambulance. We'll mount up and take back trails west to the Wind Rivers."

West stared down at the ground for a moment. "Does the Lieutenant know that country? I mean ... well, I don't. And I don't think the others do."

"I know it."

Even as he said it, Brian knew he was telling less than the truth. He had been told of a trail across the end of the Wind River Mountains, but that was years ago. How much did he remember?

Off the point of the mountain there was a settlement, but they dared not go there. It was a small settlement, a few people only. It would mean disaster for them if he tried to take refuge there, for even less than the wagon train could they defend themselves against what Kelsey would bring upon them.

West was not satisfied. "Lieutenant, it is a big risk ... with all that money."

"You have a solution to suggest, Corporal?"

West looked angry. "It isn't my place to tell you what to do, sir. You're in command. That's what you told us when you took us away from the wagon train, and I ain't sure that was such a good idea."

"What has been done was done by me and is my responsibility, Corporal. Now if you have an alternative to suggest I shall be only too happy to hear it. Otherwise, enough has been said. Do you have such a plan?"

"No, but—"

Ironhide appeared suddenly in the cut. "Riders, sir. I'd guess about thirty of them."

Scrambling up the cut after Ironhide, rocks rolling under his feet, Ten Brian knew the trouble he had feared was here. Deep down, he had never really believed they could escape Kelsey—not without a fight.

West had followed them up, and now he crouched beside Brian, watching the riders coming.

They rode in a column of two's, led by a big man on a blood bay. Ironhide pointed, and for the first time

31

Brian saw two other men, scouting well ahead of the column, cutting back and forth, looking for signs.

Most of the men wore buckskins. Through his glasses, which he kept down behind a masking bush to prevent any reflection from them, Brian saw that the one thing all had in common was excellence of horseflesh and horsemanship.

"Are those the men?" West's tone was reluctant.

"Yes—and take a good look. I know Kelsey, and you can be sure there isn't a man in that outfit who hasn't been carefully chosen—for fighting ability, at least."

"And you think they wiped out the wagon train?"

"Yes, I do. My information was that they had been destroying wagon trains for over a year. Their secret of success has been that they have allowed no one to escape."

"Except us and our ambulance."

"And therefore they must find it, and us. You may be sure of this: that Reuben Kelsey will stop at nothing to destroy us all. As long as nothing is known of him he can operate in perfect freedom, choosing what targets he will, and when he will, without fear of pursuit or risk of getting involved."

The column rode past. They had come no nearer than about three hundred yards, and fortunately, nowhere near the trail by which Brian's men had approached their hide-out, but Brian was worried. Did Kelsey realize he was with the command. How much had he told Kelsey about his hiding place at that meeting long ago on the Sweetwater—how he had waited here while the Indians searched all around but had not found him?

Leaving Ironhide on lookout, he went down the cut. "All right," he said to the men, "saddle the horses, strip the ambulance. We're moving out."

They worked swiftly. Blankets, slickers, food, medical supplies, ammunition, and the sixty thousand dollars in gold—all were taken care of. Aside from what they could carry in their saddlebags and behind the cantles, two pack horses would be used.

Within an hour they were moving out. Ten Brian took the lead, pointing his horse north into the wilderness, and the others followed, reluctantly.

Turning in his saddle, he glanced back once. He kept them to low ground in single file, and twice he led the way across great slabs of rust-red rock. Then he went back and, after smudging out the marks made by the horseshoes, he took up dust in his fingers and let it sift over the rock where they had passed. Ironhide brought up the rear. He trusted the Cherokee to watch the back trail.

They were taking a chance in going north, for there would be no likelihood of help there, but it was the last direction their pursuers would expect. Also, it would be easier to cover their trail, and there was a route over the mountains and down the western slope.

If worse came to worst, he would turn back, find Kelsey, and kill him.

With Kelsey dead, the others might scatter, for none of them had his will, his drive.

Chapter 5

Turpenning rode back to the column, and Major Devereaux halted the troops and dismounted them for a few minutes rest before going on.

"Suh"—Turpenning squatted on the ground so that he could draw in the dirt—"I picked up their sign. The Lieutenant, suh, he's a foxy one. He figures he's followed, suh, an' he's doin' his level best to leave no trail. With an ambulance that's hard . . . almighty hard.

"Them renygades, they're a-huntin' him—men scattered out to all sides, cuttin' for sign." Turpenning chuckled. "A couple of times they cut right acrost his trail without findin' hide nor hair."

"How far behind them are the renegades?"

"An hour . . . mebbe two. The Lieutenant, suh, he's uncommon shrewd. They'll have themselves a time comin' up to him." Turpenning paused, chewing on a blade of grass. "Major, suh, a body a-readin' sign sometimes figures things beyond a few scratches in the sand. A body surmises, suh."

"And what do you surmise?"

"The Lieutenant, suh, he's scared."

"Frightened? Lieutenant *Brian?*"

"No, suh. Not scared thataway, but scared wary, suh, if you get what I mean. Lieutenant Brian, suh, is worried about who's on his trail. He ain't just tryin' to

34

leave no sign; he's doin' partic'lar things. He's actin' like he knows somebody's on his trail who ain't about to give up.

"Suh, if you-all don't mind, I figure to be an uncommon good tracker. I growed up with Injuns, an' you let me follow a man's trail long enough an' I'll read you his life story, like. There's nothin' like a trail to show character in a body. Well, suh, Lieutenant Brian I've tracked before this—"

"For what reason?"

Turpenning shrugged. "Nature, I s'pect. You all give a beaver some sticks an' water an' he'll build hisself a dam. You give me a trail, an' I'll follow it. Also"—he spat—"if'n I'm to trust my life to a man, I'm wishful to know what manner of man he is.

"Well, suh, Lieutenant Brian, suh, just naturally he gives you nothin' to take hold of. Even with troops, suh. He don't just ride off acrost the country, suh, he *knows* the lay of land like he'd shaped it with his own hands ... no Injun is ever goin' to ambush him. And they know it, suh."

He paused, spat again. "I've heerd 'em talkin', suh. He's a most admired man, a big warrior. You ever want anybody to make palaver with Injuns, you send him. They know him an' they respect him."

"Let's get back to the trail," Devereaux said. He had known that Brian was a good soldier, but that the Indians knew him so well and respected him so much he had not suspected.

"Ain't much more I can tell, except what I figure. Brian's headed for Bridger, sure as shootin', an' he knows somebody's on his trail that wants him almighty bad, somebody he knows or knows about."

Devereaux studied the marks in the sand, considered the country before him and the time he had left, measuring hours of travel against rations, and he was dismayed. There was so little time. He discounted Turpenning's ideas about Brian fearing a known enemy,

35

but he knew too much about scouting to discount much else Turpenning said.

"What do you think he will do?" he asked Turpenning.

"Ain't no doubt, knowin' the Lieutenant. He's goin' to leave that ambulance, mount 'em all a-horseback, an' head for wild country."

"You think he won't run for it?"

"No, suh. He'd get ketched, and he knows it. Anyway, suh, the Lieutenant's a man who'll use savvy before he uses fightin' or runnin'. He'll run if need be, and fight if he's ketched, but he'll try to lose 'em. I'd guess, suh, that he'll head into the Wind River Mountains."

"Why?"

"Wild country, suh. Hidin' places. He can travel for miles under cover of canyons or brush. You could hide an army up there, suh, and he knows it."

"Major," Cahill said, about Lieutenant Brian knowing his enemy, sir. He knows Reuben Kelsey, sir."

"Kelsey?" Devereaux spoke impatiently. "Lieutenant, Reuben Kelsey is in Kansas or Missouri, or perhaps in Kentucky."

"Do we know that, sir? Kelsey knows this part of the country, and where could he cause more trouble than here? Begging your pardon, sir, but Lieutenant Brian's family were killed by the Indians within a few miles of here. Kelsey's folks were killed at the same time. They met after the massacre and made their way back to Laramie together."

"That's all supposition, Lieutenant. We have no reason to think Kelsey is out here at all. In fact, he is generally believed to have been killed."

"Yes, sir. It was just a thought, sir."

Turpenning had been listening. "That would explain somethin', suh. That Kelsey now—he's a big man, I hear."

36

"He is. About six-two, and he weighs around two hundred and forty pounds," Cahill replied.

"Well, suh, this man who leads them renygades makes a deeper track than any man in our outfit. He's a big man, suh—easy on his feet, but heavy."

"Nonsense! Kelsey operates in the East. Forget him and get down to business." He straightened up. "Mount your men, Cahill. We're going to try to catch up. If we do, we'll go into battle. Maybe we can pin them down, and if we can't we can hold them up long enough for Brian to escape, if that is what he is trying to do."

When Turpenning had gone Cahill said, "Then you don't suspect Lieutenant Brian?"

"Lieutenant Cahill, Lieutenant Brian's post is at Fort Laramie, the term of his leave has expired or is about to expire, and he is proceeding in the opposite direction. He has assumed command, on his own initiative, of an army ambulance and a detachment under special orders, and he has caused that detachment to leave its prescribed line of march."

"And in so doing," Cahill suggested, "he has saved your daughter's life."

"And also," Major Devereaux replied, "taken an army payroll of sixty thousand dollars."

Cahill was astounded. *"Sixty thousand?* Sir, I had no idea!"

"I understand that, Lieutenant. I hope you will also consider the fact that Lieutenant Brian, no matter how efficient as an officer, is also a foot-loose adventurer with no known ties, and that such a sum of money has been a temptation to men with more secure relationships.

"I repeat, Lieutenant, I suspect nobody. I am merely considering all the possibilities. You recognize the fact that some explanations are in order, do you not?"

"Yes, sir," Cahill admitted, "I do."

Major Mark Devereaux scanned the area as they moved forward. It was exhilarating. The air was fresh

37

and cool, the country already had the greenish cast of new grass growing. He walked his command for a short distance, then cantered for half a mile.

Turpenning, with two men, was ranging far ahead to provide warning when they sighted the renegades.

Major Devereaux eased in the saddle. Advancing years had not increased his weight, and he now weighed two pounds less than on the day he married, a fact of which he was proud, but which he never mentioned. Though his income was not large, his uniforms were tailored by the best tailor he could find; and no man at any post where he had served could recall seeing him unshaved.

Several times he had been offered staff positions that might have led to promotion, but he preferred the field. As he grew older the opportunities grew fewer. Staff positions, he noticed, were given more often to easier men, men less abrasive than himself. Generals had a way of wanting men about them who were easy to be with, and whose efficiency would not make them uncomfortable.

Lieutenant Tenadore Brian, he thought, might be an exception to that rule. He had a way of being damn good at whatever he was doing, without being obtrusive about it. Handsome as he was, and with his background of travel, it was a wonder he had not become an attaché at some embassy.

Major Devereaux said as much to Cahill. "Oh, he wouldn't have it, sir," Cahill replied. "I happen to know from other sources that he was offered something of the kind. He's like yourself, sir, he prefers the frontier, and active soldiering."

After a moment he added, "He speaks five or six languages, sir, and reads them as well."

"That's not altogether unusual," Devereaux commented, "I've learned never to be surprised at the men I meet on the frontier. The first sergeant of Company K of the First Cavalry was a Russian nobleman, and we have a man in this outfit who was an officer in the Austrian army."

"Is that so?" Cahill was intrigued. "Now, who would that be?"

Devereaux smiled. "I will leave that one to puzzle you, Lieutenant. He doesn't want anyone to know, and has no idea that I do."

"How did you find out?"

"Remember that viscount who reviewed the troops before they came west? That was his brother. He told me in confidence."

They fell silent, hearing only the beat of hoofs on the turf, as the dust rose from the thin grass.

Mark Devereaux was thinking of Mary. Where was she now? Was she frightened? Oddly, for all his dislike of Ten Brian, he was reassured by the thought that she was with him. Whatever one might think of him, he had always conducted himself as a gentleman. He remembered something he had heard the man say when an officer of another unit had resigned his commission over a love affair with a prostitute.

"Right or wrong," Brian had said flatly, "I respect him for his action. He respects the woman, and that is as it should be. Any woman I am with"—he paused a moment—"would be treated as a lady, no matter who or what she was."

Damn it all, Devereaux said to himself, *when there is so much about the man that I respect, why do I dislike him?*

They were gaining on the renegades. Even Devereaux could see the increasing freshness of the tracks. Did they know they were pursued? He asked himself that question and could come to no conclusion. So far there was no indication of any change of route.

Twice he halted the column for short breaks, each time choosing a spot with cover and some shade. At the

39

second stop he ordered coffee, and while the men drank it he listened to Turpenning's report.

"It'll be dark in an hour, suh, but they've gone into camp. Built theirselves some fires, and settled down like they figured to have themselves a time."

"Guards posted?"

"Yes, suh. Leastways they taken position. I got close enough for that. Picked theirselves some good spots, good cover, and all the country a body would want to look over."

Devereaux studied the Tennessean thoughtfully. "What's the matter, Turpenning? Is there something about it you don't like?"

"Yes, suh. There surely is. Somethin' about it feels wrong, you see? Like maybe they've got that ambulance treed, or somethin' up their sleeves. I can't put a finger on what's wrong, but it's surely there."

"All right. I'll accept your word." He knew too much about such men not to recognize their sensitivity to a situation. He had had the same feeling himself on several occasions, and had ignored it to his cost.

"Turpenning," he said now, "you need rest and I want you to get it. At the same time I need a report on that camp, and I need a couple of men who could scout around and see if they do have the ambulance pinned down. You've worked with a good many of my men. Who would you suggest?"

Devereaux had his own ideas, but the Tennessean had worked with most of the outfit, and he wanted his opinion.

"Well, suh, with Gogarty gone—and he was one of the best—there's Chancel, Boner, and Halleck, all three good men."

Devereaux was startled. Stub Boner had been a hunter, Halleck was a soldier who had served in Dakota and Wisconsin, knew Indians and their ways, and spoke several tongues . . . but Chancel?

40

Turpenning answered the question before it was asked. "You might be a-wonderin' about Chancel," he said; "but the man's knowin', suh, mighty knowin'. His ears is uncanny good, an' he don't waste no moves. He's got less experience in this country, but a-plenty when it comes to savvy. I been on the scout with him a couple of times, an' I fit Injuns alongside him. He shoots careful, wastes no lead, and never shoots until he's got him a target dead in his sights."

"Thank you, Turpenning. Now get yourself some more coffee and then catch some sleep. You're apt to need it."

He sipped his own coffee, making it last. Well, one never knew. Chancel was the Austrian lieutenant, now a corporal. He sent for him.

Corporal Chancel carried himself well. He was a lean, compact man, an excellent horseman and rifle shot. His military background became apparent soon after he joined up, and also his natural gift for leadership. The men liked him, respected his knowledge, and his lack of desire to impress.

"Chancel," Major Devereaux said, "I want you to go on the scout." He indicated the area. "I want you to go around the renegade camp. Be careful, for some of those men are woodsmen from birth. Swing around and see if you can find the ambulance or any of our people. Unless there is some development we won't move from here until almost daybreak, when we go into the camp. Report to me, and if I am not available, to Lieutenant Cahill."

"Yes, sir."

"And Corporal, remember that whoever is in command over there is no fool."

"No, sir. All right, sir."

Twice he climbed the gentle slope to look in the direction of the renegade camp. The fires were burning brightly, and the first time he thought he saw move-

41

ment about them. The second time he saw nothing but the fires. He would wait until the last hour before dawn, and then move in.

He had dozed off when a hand shook him. "Sir, they've fooled us. They're gone."

Chapter 6

"Gone?"

"Yes, sir." It was Halleck who had awakened him. "It was no camp, sir . . . just the fires. Turp could tell better than me, but I'd say they left two or three men behind to keep the fires going and show some movement about. Then they just slipped away."

"Thank you, Halleck. Is Chancel back?"

"No, sir, and it's coming on for day. I am worried, sir, him being a foreigner, and all."

"Private Halleck, at least thirty per cent of this command is forcign, as you put it. And some of our best men are among them."

When he was gone, Devereaux considered the possibilities for a few moments, then he lay down, pulled his blankcts around him, and fell promptly to sleep. A good soldier eats when there is food, never stands when he can sit, and never stays awake when he can sleep . . . as long as it doesn't interfere with his duty.

He was awakened by the smell of wood burning, and saw Turpenning squatted beside a fire he had recently kindled. The coffeepot was on a rock in the center of the flames.

"Mornin', suh. I been out for a look-see."

"Yes?"

"No camp . . . just a blind. They pulled out fast.

43

This here was to hold you whilst they got away. And they're onto somethin', suh. They found some sign, but noways enough."

"What do you mean by that?"

"Well, suh, those boys are mighty handy, but they sure ain't found any kind of a trail. The way they're scoutin' the country, they ain't rightly sure what happened. Whatever they found, they lost. That Lieutenant Brian, suh, he's a cagey one."

"How many men do they have?"

"Nigh onto forty. That's a sort of guess, but I figured by the rifle stacks an' the length of the picket line for their horses."

"You found their camp, then?"

"Yes, suh. They built up those fires, an' then they pulled their freight. They went on about four, five mile up the country and made a dark camp. They hadn't been gone no more'n thuty minutes when I come upon it."

"Is Chancel back?"

"No, suh. Not hide nor hair."

"Thank you, Turpenning. I'll have that coffee now."

He would gain on them during the day. The fact that they had to find a trail would restrict their movements. This they would understand as well as he, and they would know he would catch up . . . hence an ambush.

It was the logical step. They could not escape him and find the fugitives, too, so they would attempt an ambush to inflict casualties and make him more cautious.

As he was finishing his breakfast, Chancel appeared.

"Fill your cup, Chancel, and sit down," he said. "I'll have your report."

"Yes, sir. I found the ambulance, sir." Without waiting for comment, he continued. "Very well hidden, sir, in a copse almost impossible to find. It was the grazing where the horses cropped grass—that helped.

"They had a lookout posted and they sighted the

44

enemy, stripped the ambulance of food and whatever they could use, mounted the horses, and left."

"Any sign of the women?"

"Yes, sir. Two of them, sir. I found their trail, followed it as far as a stream, then lost it."

"Had others found the trail?"

"Yes, sir. I think they lost it, too."

Brian would try for Bridger, of course. By now that was evident. It would also be evident to the renegades, who would attempt to overtake them or cut them off. Brian knew this country—but how well did he know it?

"Sir?"

"What is it, Chancel?"

"The enemy, sir. They know this country. Know it well. Several times they rode the easiest way . . . but it was not always the easiest to find. Their leader knows what he is about, sir."

Mark Devereaux was not a man who hurried, and even now, with time and distance a matter of the greatest importance, he took his time, trying to figure out what procedures they might adopt.

All possible positions of ambush would have to be scouted, but these renegades had lived among Indians, and Indians had a way of choosing a spot for ambush in the last place one would suspect.

Devereaux rode up on the knoll with Turpenning and Chancel and studied the country while they pointed out its features. He swept the country carefully with his glasses, and then examined it at a closer range.

Cahill rode up to join him, and Devereaux explained briefly the situation as it might develop. "We must guard against surprise. Be especially careful in what seems to be open country. I want to pin them down and get them into a fire fight."

He turned. "Now, Chancel, take me to the ambulance, and I'll take Halleck along. Cahill, form up and move out, but get Turpenning and Boner well out in front. Use them, but don't rely only on them."

45

With Chancel leading the way, they rode swiftly. As they neared the copse where the ambulance had been hidden Devereaux studied the terrain. The camp was small, and the ambulance was not visible at all until one was within a dozen feet of it. It would have to be snaked out, of course, and brought back. It would be useful in the event of wounded men.

He went at once to the secret compartment. The gold was gone . . . but he had expected that. Nevertheless, it had been his duty to see for himself. He walked up to higher ground. From here they could easily have seen the approach of the renegades and they would have had time to escape if they moved swiftly.

"Took me a time to find this place, sir," Chancel said. "It was not a simple thing."

"I can see that." Devereaux was studying the land as he spoke. He looked thoughtfully at the Wind River range, looming up to the west. "I wonder if there's any way over that," he said.

"Yes, sir," Halleck said. "It isn't easy, but a mountain man at Fort Laramie told me it could be done."

The South Pass country, which lay before them, was open after they passed the Beaver Rim. Broken country quickly petered out into rolling plains. A small group heading southwest for Fort Bridger would have a bad time of it. What would Brian do?

By mid-afternoon they had not come up to the renegades, and time was growing short. When they took a brief halt, Devereaux stepped down from the saddle and his knees sagged a little. For a moment he stood still, getting hold of himself. There was a limit to what a man could do, he supposed, but he must be careful to show no weakness.

After a moment he walked to a flat rock and sat down. Shadows were gathering in the mouths of the canyons. What sunlight there was touched the remaining spots of snow high on the mountains. The air was cool, and amazingly fresh. Far off toward the west he could see several objects moving along the shoulder of a hill. He leveled his glasses ... buffalo, half a dozen of them.

It was late, and the buffalo would probably bed down somewhere in the vicinity. If the situation permitted, he might send several men out to get them. The buffalo meat would augment their rations, and might give him another day in which to work. Saving the payroll would be a permissible excuse for remaining out from the Fort that much longer.

Turpenning and Halleck came in together. "Found them, suh," Turpenning said with satisfaction. "They're camped under the Beaver Rim, only a few miles from here. They followed Twin Creek and skirted the foot of Limestone Mountain yonder. They're camped in a meadow about three-quarters of a mile below the Rim."

"The trail they followed—is it guarded?"

"You just bet it is, suh! They got them four men staked out there, a-watchin' for us. But Halleck an' me, we scouted around some, an' we come on a game trail down the face of the rim."

"Can we make it?"

"Uh-huh. I mean, yes, suh. That there rim's about five hundred feet high, and she drops sheer from the top for maybe seventy-five, eighty feet, but there's a trail. It ain't for skittish folks, but we can make it."

"Did you try it?"

"I did, sir," Halleck said. "I went down, all the way to Beaver Creek at the bottom. I went a-foot, sir, but horses will have no trouble."

Here it was then. It might be an ambush, but they must risk it. A hard blow now might take the pressure off Brian, might give him just the chance needed to make a run for Bridger or to hole up somewhere in the mountains. He could settle with Brian afterward. It was a case of first things first.

He turned to Cahill, "Lieutenant," he said, "give the men a hot meal. Pickets out, and good men. I want no slip-ups now. About four hours sleep, and we'll move out shortly after midnight."

He thought of Mary. Where was she? What was she doing now? Belle was with her, fortunately, and for all her flighty looks, Belle was Army. She had seen her husband through a dozen campaigns, and she had made some long, hard treks herself.

He got out his razor, heated water over the fire, and shaved by the last light. As he shaved he considered the steps that must be taken.

He would have to move with care, for these were woodsmen, Indian fighters, far more skilled at fighting than most of his own men. But even such men can become careless, and they knew his troops were green.

Putting his kit away, he stretched out on his blanket, slowly easing his tired muscles. He smelled bacon frying and the smell of coffee, mixed with the smell of cedar. He could think this was a good life ... if only Mary were safe.

Ten Brian stepped down from the saddle and walked back to Mary, holding up his hands to help her down. "We'll rest here," he said, and turned to help Belle from the saddle.

Ironhide and Schwartz got down immediately, then Dorsey. Only West lingered in the saddle, looking around carefully.

"What river is that?" he asked.

"The Popo Agie," Brian said; "actually what they call the Little Popo Agie. Better get down and get some rest. You're going to need it tomorrow."

Unwillingly, West got down. He was as tired as the others, but he was increasingly wary. The more he thought of it the less he trusted Lieutenant Brian.

Brian was a good soldier, admitted, but how had he happened to ride up out of nowhere and order them off the wagon train? He should have refused.

Brian said the wagon train had been wiped out, but

48

he admitted he had not seen it done. The whole thing might be a cock-and-bull story to get them back in the hills where nobody would ever find them, and murder the lot of them. Sixty thousand dollars was a lot of money.

He got down warily, keeping his horse between Brian and himself. Thoughtfully, he considered the others. At least one of them might be an ally of Brian. Ironhide had served with him, and Ironhide was an Indian, and after all, you couldn't trust an Indian, even an educated one like Ironhide.

"Schwartz, fix us a good meal," Brian said. He spoke over his shoulder while going from one horse to the other, checking their backs for sore spots, and looking them over with care.

Mary walked down to the stream, where thick groves of cottonwood grew right down to the bank. As she stood looking into the clear water, Brian came down, cut himself a willow pole, and baited his hook with bacon rind. Within minutes he had landed a speckled trout.

"Have we gotten away, Ten?" Mary asked.

"No. I won't lie to you, Mary. We're in serious trouble. Right now I'd say we have a few hours. Kelsey has lost our trail, but he'll find it, and he'll come on fast. Or he may elect to go on toward Fort Bridger, scatter pickets across the country where we must travel, and just wait. He knows we have to come that way."

"So how can we escape?"

"I don't think he can hold his men out here very long. We're going up over the divide. We may have to change, but I think we'll cut through Sweetwater Gap, come down off the mountain, and go straight across the valley to the other side. If we can manage it without being seen we'll cross the Green and then make a run for it down the far side. I think we'll have a chance. But he's a devil . . . we can't low-rate him . . . not for a minute."

49

Belle Renick had come down to the stream to join them, and she was listening to him. "It's too bad," she said, "that we couldn't have come to this place under other conditions. It's beautiful."

Brian hauled in his fourth trout, and rebaited the hook. "It is," he said, "and you'll see more of it tomorrow. The Wind River Mountains have some of the finest glaciers you'll find anywhere, and some lovely lakes."

He went on talking and Mary listened, but she was hearing more than the words; she was sensing something of the man behind them. Tenadore Brian was, she thought, one of the most attractive men she had ever met . . . not the most handsome, although he was very good-looking, but there was something in his presence that said more than words. He talked easily, and having traveled and studied, above all having thought about what he had seen and read, he had much to talk about.

She knew he was talking in part to put them at ease. It had been a hard, dangerous day. So far they had eluded their pursuers . . . if there were any. She herself had seen no enemies, but she knew enough of the frontier to know she had seen a classic job of evasion and escape.

Brian had led them over a shelf of rock and into the water. They had gone downstream for half a mile before he led them out through tall grass. He had gone back alone and carefully brushed the grass back into position so that a casual glance would show no evidence of their passing. Then from rock shelf to stream, and stream to rock shelf, they had worked their way across and up the mountain, angling back and forth by a switchback route until they had stopped for noon among some rocks. From that vantage point he had studied both their back trail for pursuit and the route they must select for climbing the mountain.

Mary had climbed up beside him, and he pointed out landmarks. "See? That is Roaring Fork Mountain, and the peaks just on the left are the Sweetwater Needles. We're going up there."

"Is there a trail?"

"An Indian trail, if we can find it. And there are a couple of passes that will let us cross over. It won't be easy, and it's going to be cold up there."

"I'm worried about pa."

"The Major? You needn't. He's a tough old campaigner."

"But Ten, he isn't as young as he was, and he won't give up. I am afraid he'll overdo it. He'll be worried about me, and I know he wasn't planning to come this far west. He will be overdue at the post, and they will be worried, too."

Brian shrugged. "Trust him. He's lived with bad situations all his life, as you should know. A man can get information and education at any age; you only get wisdom with experience, and he has it." He paused. "I just wish he knew that was Reuben Kelsey down there. It would make all the difference."

Nothing appeared below. For a long time, keeping his glasses in shadow so no sun could reflect from them, he studied the terrain, not only along his back trail, but off to the southeast where the pursuers were more likely to be.

Corporal West had moved off to one side of the camp with Dorsey. They were gathering wood. West stood up for a moment, hands on hips. "I don't like it," he said to Dorsey.

"What?"

"There's no reason for us to be away off up here. What's Brian think he's doing, anyway?"

"Gettin' away. What else? When you're protectin' two handsome women and sixty thousand in gold—isn't that what you said?—well, you got to think."

"Nevertheless, I don't like it."

Dorsey glanced toward camp. Nobody was within hearing. "Do you think he plans to steal that gold?"

"I don't know what to think."

"You could always make sure."

West looked at him. "How do you mean?"

"Take the gold and run for it. Head for Bridger right now. Or head for Major Devereaux. He's somewhere close behind."

West wet his lips, and shifted his feet uneasily. The thought had occurred to him.

"If that's what you decide to do, West, you can count me in," Dorsey said almost casually. "I'll back you in whatever you decide."

"Thanks." The money was really in West's charge, not Brian's. Brian wasn't even supposed to know about the money. This was West's duty. And now here they were far off up in the mountain. They had left no trail for the renegades, but nothing for the army, either. He said as much to Dorsey.

"That's right," Dorsey agreed, "right now nobody but us knows where we are or where that money is."

"It's my responsibility," West said.

"Well, I'd say if anything happened to it, you'd be held responsible all right." After a moment he added, "If a body was to go right off the end of this mountain he would be heading about right. Bridger is southwest from here."

And the Oregon Trail, Dorsey reminded himself, *takes off to the northwest.*

"All right," West said, "we'll watch our chance."

"That we will," Dorsey replied, "that we will, Corporal."

Chapter 7

Their fire was small and was built with dry sticks. It gave off almost no smoke, and with the wind as it was whatever smoke there was would be drawn down the canyon of the Popo Agic.

After less than an hour of fishing, Brian had pulled in a dozen good-sized trout. The glade in which they had chosen to camp was sheltered from the little wind, and after the long day it was restful there by the swift-running water.

"What bird is that?" Mary asked suddenly, pointing. The bird was slate gray, its head brown. It was perched on a rock, its head bobbing.

"We call it a dipper," Brian said, "because of the way he dips his head, but properly he's a water ouzel. Watch him . . . he'll dive right in, walk around on the bottom of the stream picking up food, and when he comes out he's dry . . . oil in his feathers, I guess. They like fast-running water, and they seem to like people, too. Anyway, I've watched them for hours and they never seem to mind."

"You're interested in birds?"

"In everything. You have to be in this country. If you know the habits of birds and animals you can tell if anyone is around, just by the way they conduct themselves."

"But what about us? Doesn't our being here affect them at all?"

"Yes, but we've been quiet, no sudden moves ... we're part of the picture. If you are in the forest and you remain quiet, birds and animals accept you. Oh, they'll keep an eye on you, but if you show no disposition to trouble them they will take you on your own terms. If anybody else comes up, off they go. And you are warned."

Night gathered around the trees and rocks, gathered in the draws and the canyons, and stretched out to the somber peaks, the only spots of brightness the snow on the summits.

Their supper was eaten. The small fired glowed from red coals. West sat in silence beyond it, while Dorsey leaned on an elbow, staring at the coals. Schwartz was on guard, and the Cherokee was dozing.

"I wish the Captain could see me now," Belle commented. "He told me it would be an easy ride to California in that ambulance. 'Just like sitting in your rocker,' he said." She turned to look at Brian. "Ten, I ask you: is there really a way over the mountain?"

"Several. The quickest and easiest is probably Sioux Pass, which cuts off to the southwest. There's Sweet-water Gap, which we may use; and then there's a pass between the peaks further along that the Shoshones and Utes used when they used to visit each other."

Brian sat up and leaned back against a rock, eyes half closed. He heard the water, and heard in memory the campfire talk of other trips, but all the while his ears were alert for sounds beyond their circle.

He was tired. His muscles loved the rest, but his mind was feeling out a way for the following day. He was letting his mind explore the mountain they would encounter tomorrow, trying to foresee what awaited them up there.

They had not lost Reuben Kelsey. Not with two women and sixty thousand dollars. Kelsey would guess

54

they had gone over the mountain even though he found no trail. He might have men among his group who knew this mountain, and knew how they must cross it. And Kelsey had only to skirt the mountain, watch and wait for them on the other side.

So far the women were bearing up well, but from now on it would be climbing, rough going over narrow trails, used only by Indians or wild game.

By now Major Devereaux would have turned back or would be preparing to do so, for he would have reached the limit of his ration allowance.

The field ration was normally three-quarters of a pound of side meat—bacon or salt pork, and more often the latter, a pound of hardtack, and a little coffee and salt. The Major may have augmented that by a little judicious hunting. There were usually buffalo and antelope on the plains, though not always when they were needed.

Ten Brian had rations enough, with a little fishing to help out if there was time. The ambulance had been equipped with food supplies to take the women through to the Coast, and for the escort as far as Fort Halleck, in Nevada.

He got up suddenly, and with a brief word walked out of camp to where Schwartz was on guard. "Anything?" Brian asked.

"Nothing, sir. Something down there in the brush, but it's an animal. Bear, probably, but not a big one."

"Been out in this country long, Schwartz?"

"I came out in fifty-eight. I could not speak the language, so I had joined the army. When this year ends I shall leave the army and go into business. I've learned the language, and I've saved my money. It is a good country, this. I shall stay here."

"Have you ever been to Fort Bridger?"

"Yes, sir. Twice . . . but never from this direction."

"If anything happens to me, get down off the mountain and head west for the Green, cross it if you can,

55

then head south for Bridger, keeping the western mountains for a background."

He went on, "And keep a sharp lookout. These men can move like Indians, Schwartz. Many of them have lived with Indians, have hunted and fought with them."

"I know their kind, sir."

Brian left him and went back to camp. Several times in the night he added fuel to the fire. He watched Dorsey move out to relieve Schwartz, and saw the German come in quietly.

At daybreak he was up and moving. A quick breakfast, and they saddled their horses. The mountain lay before them.

Ten Brian led off, weaving a way among the pines, then, through a grove of aspen. He wasted no time trying to cover the trail, simply riding through unlikely places, cutting across to the trail he wanted, south of Brown's Gulch. By mid-morning they were at Cold Spring, looking south toward the Freak Mountains which cut off their view of what lay to the south.

He rode with his Winchester in his hand, for there was no telling what lay ahead of them. By now Kelsey would have a good idea what he was attempting and might try to cut him off, and there was always the danger of Indians. Shoshones and Utes used these trails, and so did the Sioux; occasionally the Blackfeet or Cheyennes passed through on raids along the Overland or Oregon trails. However, he saw no signs of recent travel.

Less than half a mile beyond Cold Spring they turned left. The trail grew worse. They rode single file, and Brian could rarely see more than one or two of the others.

They had gone no more than a mile when suddenly the trail vanished. They had emerged upon the very lip of a steep cliff, which fell at least a thousand feet to

56

Canyon Creek. Mary came up alongside him, her face pale.

"We're going down *that?*"

"Just sit your horse. She'll take you down. That's a good mare."

He took out his glasses and studied the country below. If they were caught on the cliff ... The north slope of Freak Mountain was covered with a thick stand of timber. An ambush might be hidden there, but it was a risk they must take.

"Ironhide," he said, "you bring up the pack horses and take the lead. Schwartz, you be the rear guard."

"What about you, sir?" West asked.

"I'm going to scout on ahead. If I remember what I was told, there's another trail comes in from around Freak Mountain and joins ours a couple of miles along. I want to scout that trail before you people get there. Come along steady, Ironhide, but don't rush it."

He turned to Mary and Belle, who were looking down the steep cliff. "Don't worry," he said. "The trail's not as bad as it looks. Just let your horses find their own way ... they'll follow those ahead."

Swinging his gray horse, he went over the rim and started down. Ironhide waited a moment, then followed.

"Are you scared, Belle?" Mary asked.

"Of course, but I've been scared before. Let's go."

They could glimpse Brian, on ahead. Mary realized she had never known anybody quite like him, and the thought of him disturbed her. She knew her father did not approve of him, yet several times he had spoken of Brian with approbation. At least twice he had handled difficult situations with Indians without getting into a fight. He showed good judgment, but ... She couldn't make up her mind.

Dorsey pushed close to West. "When?" he whispered.

"We'll try for Sioux Pass," West said after a moment. "Wait for me to lead off."

"How can we? When Ironhide has the money?"

"Leave that to me," West replied. "He won't always have it."

West did not relish the idea of breaking away from Ten Brian. He did not really trust him, but neither did he want to go against him. He had never seen Brian angry, but he could imagine what it might be like.

Once at the bottom of the trail, Ten Brian let his gray have its head. After half a mile he slowed up. The trail was closing in and he could see only a few yards ahead. He moved carefully, studying the trail for tracks, but he saw only deer or elk tracks. Once he saw that a huge bear had crossed the trail. His horse snorted a little, not liking the smell, which apparently lingered.

A fork in the trail appeared and he drew up, scanning the shallow basin where the trails met. He took several minutes to study the trees and brush on all sides, then walked his horse slowly forward. There was little time, for the others would be coming.

Suddenly, he glimpsed the tracks of two riders. They had come in from the southeast, skirting the foot of Freak Mountain, and they had stopped here, then turned back. Apparently they had looked for tracks, and finding none had done an about-face.

"All right, soldier boy," a voice said, "drop your rifle."

He saw them then, down the trail, just back in the trees. Both of them had rifles, but he did not hesitate. His left hand held the reins, his right held the rifle by the action, its barrel lying across the bend of his left elbow where he had been letting it rest as he looked about. He tilted the rifle and fired.

Once . . . twice . . .

They had been sure—too sure. And his movement had been slight, almost undetectable at forty yards. At his second shot he slammed the spurs to the gray and leaped him at them.

One man was down, his foot caught in the stirrup; the other was wounded, and was clutching the pommel of his saddle, his face gray with fright.

"Don't," he whispered hoarsely, "don't shoot no more!"

"Are you Kelsey's men?"

The man nodded. "He'll kill you for this," he said. "He'll hear those shots."

Pushing his mount close, Brian flipped the six-shooter from the man's belt, but saw no other weapons.

"Turn your horse," he said, "and ride to him."

"I'll never make it."

"You'd better hope you do," Brian said calmly. "And while you're riding, remember those women and children that were with the wagon train. And when you get to Kelsey, you tell him to lay off. Tell him Ten Brian sent the message."

"Brian? I've heard that name." The man was clinging tightly to the pommel. There was blood on his saddle now, a good deal of it. "I'll tell him," he said. "But he'll kill you!"

"You'd better go," was all that Brian said.

Chapter 8

A few minutes before midnight Devereaux woke and lay for a moment under his blanket considering the possible moves that lay before them.

The night was still, and on such a night the slightest noise would carry. They must move with extreme caution in going down the trail.

He had no thought of trying to surround the renegades, simply of hitting them a staggering blow. Surrounded, they would put up a hard fight, and Devereaux doubted that his men were up to it. Good men, most of them, but not as seasoned as the renegades, by all accounts. It must be a quick, hard blow, and let them try to fight their way out of it, or run. Scatter their horses if possible.

He still had not been able to capture a member of the band, but it might work out tonight. He needed information, needed it badly. Kelsey ... suppose this was Kelsey? If it was, he should capture or kill him at all costs, but he thought Kelsey would not be so far west.

Turpenning came up through the darkness and put out the remaining coals of the fire. Turpenning was always careful.

"All right, Cahill," Devereaux said. "No noise now. Turpenning, you lead off."

Here and there was a faint rattle of accoutrements, a shuffle of feet, and the column moved out. No matter how long he served, Devereaux thought, he would always feel an excitement about these night moves, the men silent, grave, moving to their horses and getting into their saddles, their bodies blotting out the stars as they passed.

With only Turpenning ahead of him, Devereaux rode into the night. They dropped off the rim, going down the trail slowly. At the bottom they forded Beaver Creek and waited there for the column to file down the mountain and assemble. By trail it was almost a mile from here to the bench on which the enemy lay, a mile of steady climb.

Turpenning and Halleck now went ahead. A few minutes only and Turpenning was back. "Don't like it, suh. Looks too quiet an' peaceful up there. All sleepin', like. One man settin' beside the fire."

"Cahill," Devereaux said, "take twenty men and move off to the left, form a line, and be ready to move in. Corporal Chancel, take ten men to the right. We'll give them a chance to surrender, but if there is any move either to resist or run, open fire."

He waited while the men filed off into the night. With the remainder of the force he moved up the center.

Suddenly Devereaux heard a man scrambling over rocks, running and gasping. He turned sharply to reprimand him but the man clutched at his arm. "Major! It's a trap! The Lieutenant said—"

He was interrupted by a wild rebel yell from somewhere out in the darkness, and in an instant a dozen torches flared and were thrown into stacks of prepared branches. Instantly the flames caught, soared, and as the light burst over the scene, there was a thunder of firing.

A bullet tugged at Devereaux's sleeve. On his right a man staggered and fell.

61

"Fire at will!" he shouted, his voice ringing out clearly. Coolly, he walked to the partial shelter of a lightning-struck tree, drawing his pistol as he went.

Turpenning, he noticed, was flat behind a rock, firing with coolness. Corporal Chancel, further to his right, had brought his ten men up to the shelter of some tumbled rocks and was directing their fire toward targets picked by the stabbing flame from guns.

Chancel would do, Devereaux told himself, for Gogarty's replacement. With his own pistol he held his fire. Suddenly a flame stabbed to his left and he lifted his gun and fired, holding low and a little to the left of the flame. He heard the clatter of a fallen rifle, and then as suddenly, the firing ceased.

For a moment there was stillness, and then he heard movement on Cahill's flank, and a sudden burst of firing. Then silence.

The bonfires were burning brightly now, showing the whole area in bright relief. "They've pulled out, suh," Turpenning said. "Hit us, an' then ran!"

"Corporal," Devereaux called to Chancel, "sweep the area. Bring me any prisoners, give me a count on the wounded and dead."

"Yes, sir."

Major Devereaux walked toward the nearest fire. He had been outguessed, but he was sure his men had not come off badly. From what he had been able to see, they had reacted well, standing up to the surprise and the fire with courage and discipline. And he had learned something more about the character of his enemy—a shrewd, daring, and capable man.

As the fire burned, he waited. Cahill was the first to report. "He was ready for us, sir, as you saw, but I think we surprised him, too. From the disposition of his men I believe he expected us to come right down the trail he followed. As it was, he had to face most of his men about and he was never able to bring most of his rifles to bear."

62

Corporal Chancel came up. "Area clear, sir. Their horses were held in readiness to run. We lost one man, and three wounded, none of them stretcher cases."

"What about the other side?"

"One man dead, sir, and we have two wounded prisoners."

Devereaux pointed toward the position at which he had fired. "Check over there, Chancel. You may find another."

Chancel went into the rocks, gun ready, then turned. "Yes, sir. One here, sir. Bullet went in under the collarbone. No exit wound."

Two then. Two less—four, counting the prisoners. It was not much, considering what remained. And the renegades had pulled out in good order. It took a strong man to enforce discipline like that on a band of outlaws.

Kelsey . . .? A possibility. If it was Kelsey that meant serious trouble.

"The prisoners, sir? You wish to talk to them?"

Cahill led the way to them. The two men had been placed near a fire. One of them was stretched out on the ground, obviously in bad shape. The other was sitting up.

The one who lay on the ground was scarcely more than a boy, and Major Devereaux felt his face grow tight. He had never had a son, but somehow seeing a boy suffer hit him hard.

The other man was partly bald, with mutton-chop sideburns, and he had quick, mean eyes. He had been shot through the upper leg, a flesh wound and possibly only a minor wound.

The boy was suffering, but he was silent, his eyes wide open, looking at nothing. Devereaux turned to the enlisted man who stood close by. "Private, get Marly up here at once, will you? That boy needs help."

"What about me?" the other prisoner demanded. "I'm shot too."

Devereaux ignored him. "When Marly comes up, have this boy moved down to the other fire, and take good care of him."

He started as if to walk away, but the prisoner spoke up again. "You bought yourself plenty of trouble, soldier boy," he sneered. "You're doin' just what we expected, an' my boys will be back."

Devereaux turned and looked at him coolly. "You think so? Do you think they will come back when there's so much at stake? In any event, it will do you no good."

He turned to Cahill. "Have one of the men bring up a rope, will you?"

"A rope?" The prisoner's voice was shrill. "What are you talkin' about? You can't hang me!"

"Why not?" Cahill fell in with the act. "We've got a rope, and there are plenty of trees."

A man came up the draw leading two mules, heavily packed. "Major, I saw a chance, sir, an' grabbed these. Figured we might be able to use the rations, sir."

Major Devereaux glanced at the mules, then at the lean, raw-boned young Irishman who was leading them. "You're Gerrity, aren't you? How did you get the mules?"

"Well, sir"—the Irishman hesitated—"we was closin' in, and there was this little draw . . . like a ditch, it was, and it came into my mind to follow it. I was thinkin' they had to have horses somewhere, an' this draw seemed to be takin' its way roundabout, sir. An' I come up to the horses. There was a mighty lot of them, but these two mules were on the end, like, an' we bein' short of rations—"

"I see, Gerrity. That was good thinking."

"Look here!" the prisoner protested. "You can't hang me! Kel—" He broke off sharply.

Cahill glanced at Devereaux. "Maybe if he told us all he knows about that bunch we could take him along with us, sir."

64

"No. Certainly not. We can't be bothered with prisoners. We haven't time for them, nor the men to guard them. Get on with it."

"Wait!" The man was desperately frightened now, as they had intended him to be. "I'll talk! I'll tell you all you want to know."

"Tell us?" Devereaux turned on him with contempt. "What could you tell us? That you're a thief and an outlaw? That you're a murderer of women and children? We know that."

"No! Now listen! I can tell you who our chief is, an' what he's figurin' on! I can tell you—"

"Your chief?" Devereaux shrugged. "Another thief like yourself . . . no more."

"That's what you think!" the man blurted. "He's Reuben Kelsey!"

So . . . there it was.

Major Devereaux took a cigar from his pocket and lit it. "Of course. We have known he was operating in this area, but ineffectually. If that's all you have to tell us, forget about it."

Obviously upset by the poor effect of his news, the man looked right and left, as if seeking some way out, but there was none.

"You wait! You just wait until he gets that money. He knows right where he can get rifles enough for the Injuns. Then you'll see!"

Devereaux took his cigar from his lips. "So that is what he hopes to do. It is a foolish idea. Rifles are not easy to come by these days."

"He knows where they are, Kelsey does. He knows where he can pick up a thousand rifles . . . brand new! And he knows what the Injuns will do to get 'em. You think you've got the world by the tail! Kelsey will have those rifles an' he'll wipe out ever' fort this side of the Mississippi!"

Chapter 9

Lieutenant Tenadore Brian had no illusions about what their chances were of making Fort Bridger, but he also knew what had to be done. They moved out at once, following the Indian trail north to Burnt Gulch.

The man he had sent back to Reuben Kelsey would find him, and deliver his message. What Kelsey would do then depended on the man's mood. Ten Brian and Reuben Kelsey had been companions as boys, in their escape from a wagon-train massacre, and in the long trek back to Fort Laramie.

Kelsey might choose to ride off and leave them alone, just for old time's sake. But Brian did not believe he would do anything of the kind. It was simply one more card he had to play, and as for the man telling where they were, Kelsey already had a good idea, and by the time he had the news they would be far from there, anyway.

It was high-country travel, meaning they had to move a little slower, and be careful of their horses. The altitude was over eight thousand feet, and at Sweet-water Gap, toward which they were pointing, it was well over ten thousand, he had heard.

They skirted Indian Ridge, and pointed toward a conical mountain ahead of them. Reaching it, they turned west again and came to a lake. The mountain terrain around them was beautiful, the air was cool off the peaks, where there was still snow. He knew he was taking a long chance, for the pass at Sweetwater Gap might be closed by snow, and if so they must turn back or try for one of the other passes further along the ridge of the Wind River Mountains.

On the shores of the lake, Brian pulled up and dismounted. "We'll rest the horses," he said.

Glancing back, he saw West and Dorsey in conversation. Schwartz was already lying down, hat over his eyes, taking advantage of the rest.

Ironhide came up to Brian. "What is the direction from here?" he asked. "I am not sure. Of these mountains I know a little, but only a little."

"We'll go west. We'll cross the Roaring Fork, skirt some pothole lakes, and follow the Middle Fork of the Popo Agie back into the gap." He paused. "There may be snow in the gap."

He went over to where Belle and Mary were seated on a drift log near the lake shore, and squatted on his heels by them. There was rich grass everywhere, gay with flowers of a dozen varieties.

"I could love this if it weren't for the circumstances," Belle commented. "I've never been so high before."

"Love it anyway," Brian said. "There are always dangers, even when you believe them to be far away. Men have lived with both danger and beauty from the beginning."

"I did not know you were a philosopher."

"Nothing of the kind. But when a man lives with a gun beside him, he comes to savor every moment if he has any sensitivity at all. The trouble is that most of us live in anticipation or in memory, never in the present moment. There must always be times like this when you just sit still and listen, feel, see. You live longer and live infinitely better."

Mary listened to him, her eyes on the country to the

67

south. He seemed so calm, so perfectly in control. Was he this way always? Her father had often said that you never really knew a man until you saw him under fire, or at least under stress.

She had heard some of the stories, for on a small army post it is hard for a man's past to be a secret, and much of Ten's military record was known. He had fought in many places, and must have known girls in most of them, but he had not married . . . at least as far as anyone knew.

After a few minutes he got up and walked back along the line, checking the horses. West was waiting for him, his face still as always, his gaze frankly suspicious. "Which way do we go from here, Lieutenant?"

"We'll go west."

"Away from Major Devereaux's command?"

"Yes." Brian paused, recognizing the man's worry. "I believe Kelsey's men are between the Major and ourselves. I think the Major is fully occupied, and perhaps he has turned back. We must not expect help."

"But isn't it better to take Sioux Pass? Isn't it closer?"

"It is. It is also the pass Kelsey is more apt to be watching."

"Those were Kelsey's men? I mean the man you killed and the other one?"

"They were."

"You understand, Lieutenant, why I am worried. After all, the money was placed in my hands. It was my responsibility."

"And now it is mine. You should be relieved, Corporal. Whatever may happen now is my fault."

"Yes, I see that. But still—"

"Don't worry, Corporal." Then Brian added, "It will be single file when we move out, and we must take it slow. We'll be climbing from now on for the rest of the day, and we must not put the horses to any undue strain."

68

After Brian had gone, Dorsey came up to West. "Well, Corporal, what are you going to do? He's heading west. That makes no sense to me."

West was thinking the same thing. Why had they come into these mountains anyway? The story about Kelsey did not ring true. As for the men, Brian had killed one of them and sent the other running, undoubtedly to die somewhere in the mountains, but were they Kelsey's men, or some unfortunate hunters he had come upon?

"Let them all start. We'll bring up the rear," West said. "And when they're strung out, we'll take off. We can be miles away before he realizes it."

"He'll come after us," Dorsey said.

"If we can't get away, we'll hide."

Dorsey shrugged. "Fine ... that's what I'd do. You're doin' the smart thing, West. Savin' sixty thousand—that's something."

Ten Brian walked back along the line. "Mount up," he said; "we're pulling out. Keep your eyes and ears open, all of you."

At the head of the column he swung into the saddle and turned his horse west toward the Roaring Fork. He glanced back once. They were all nicely strung out. He turned his horse into the trees. From now on he must depend on them to keep up, for he could see only the horse immediately behind him, and that was the way it would be much of the time as they wove through the trees.

He had no doubts about the kind of man with whom they dealt. Kelsey had been a rough and ruthless boy, quick to take advantage, glib in talking his way out of trouble, ready to fight on the instant, and prepared to use the dirtiest of tactics. He had grown into a powerful man, a leader, and one without scruples. If he chose not to follow them it would be because his whim directed otherwise, or because he had become lazy; but if he

69

found them he would have no mercy, for he had no such feeling in him.

Considering Kelsey made Brian consider himself. You might say that both had started from that wagon-train massacre long ago. Both had lost their parents and whatever backround they might have given them. What had gone before in Kelsey's life he did not know. He had known him only as another boy of his own age with the wagon train, a rough, brawling boy with whom he had little in common. His own people had been poor but energetic Irish, both of them second-generation Americans.

He thought about them now. His grandfather had landed from Ireland and not long after had gone to work as a laborer; he had fought in the last battles of the Revolutionary War, and after the war had become a stock drover. He had been murdered for money from the sale of a small herd; his son had grown up to work on the Erie Canal, and afterward migrated west to Illinois.

In 1848 they had started for California. Ten's studious inclination had been encouraged by his grandfather, but Ten had known him only as an old man, still strong and active when well into his seventies, who had told the boy stories of the Revolution, and of frontier Indian fighting.

It was after Brian had joined the French forces in Africa that a chance remark had made one of his officers realize that the young recruit had an interest in military science, and he had found occasion to talk with him and to lend him books. It was this same officer who suggested him for a battlefield commission.

Brian had gone on to fight in other wars and to win honors; but where was he today? What did he have to offer any girl but life on a series of remote outposts on the Indian frontier? Of course, he had been suggested for a diplomatic appointment, but such appointments usually went to men of independent income, for the pay of an officer in the army would scarcely enable even a single man to live in the necessary manner. And there seemed to be no future in the army. Many of the lieutenants he had met on the frontier were men advanced in years. After the Civil War there had been a surplus of officers available, and the chances of advancement were slight.

To face up to the facts, he was a man of thirty who was going exactly nowhere. It was this meeting with Mary that made him realize fully the extent of his drifting.

He abandoned these thoughts as he came to the river, which he skirted until he discovered a place where it might be forded. At this point the water was scarcely knee-deep, but it was running with a strong current.

Ironhide was waiting on the opposite shore. Brian walked the gray into the cold, swift-running water, and went on across the stream. The others followed, gathering on the low bank. Mary, Belle, and Schwartz, were there, but there was no sign of West or Dorsey.

"Schwartz, where's West?" Brian asked. "He should have been right behind you."

"He was behind me, sir, but he and Dorsey had kind of fallen back."

Brian hesitated. They were probably just lagging behind, but West had been obviously discontented. Brian had recognized that for what it was, for West had never wanted to leave the wagon train and had done so only under a direct order. He felt that West was a trustworthy man, maybe not too bright, but stubborn in his devotion to his responsibilities.

Dorsey was another kind of man altogether. He was intelligent, up to a point, but was given to overrating himself and his abilities, and looking upon other men with contempt. Brian was sure that Dorsey had been in the army before, had deserted, and re-enlisted. That was not unusual, and there was no way of checking on

71

such men. Desertion was one thing, but sixty thousand dollars was another.

"Ironhide, skirt those pothole lakes and ride on toward the pass. Camp this side of it. I'll find West and Dorsey and catch up. If anything happens to me, you know what to do."

"Yes, sir." Ironhide swung his horse and led off.

Mary held back. "I'm frightened, Ten. What if something *should* happen to you?"

"Trust Ironhide and Schwartz. They are both good men. After the pothole lakes you'll come up to Stough Creek. The Middle Fork of the Popo Agie is right beyond it. You'll follow the Middle Fork into the pass. On the other side you'll find the head of the Sweetwater."

"Must you go?"

"There's the payroll. I assumed charge and I am responsible. Those two can't have gone far."

Wheeling his horse, he plunged into the stream again. After crossing, he rode swiftly, watching for sign that would show him where they had turned off.

He found it . . . a feeble attempt had been made to cover their trail, but neither man was good at such things. Two riders and a pack horse, heading south for the Little Popo Agie basin. They were traveling fast, too fast for the condition of their horses, none of which had the stamina of his own big gray.

Emerging from the trees, he drew up to scan the countryside. There was the danger in following their trail that he might be careless about other considerations. Kelsey might have men up in here, and there was always the chance of a war party of Indians.

He saw nothing to warn him of any trouble and he moved on, holding the horse to a swift pace. He knew he could not allow himself to remain long on their trail. Ironhide and Schwartz were as trustworthy as any two men could be, and Ironhide was a good man on a trail, but Sweetwater Gap was narrow and it was too early

72

for all the snow to be gone. They would surely need help, and lives were more important than money.

Corporal West was frightened. He had been suspicious of Lieutenant Brian's motives, but without Dorsey's encouragement he would not have made the break. But this was the shortest way out of the mountains, and now it would be a hard, fast ride to Fort Bridger. If he brought this off it would mean a sergeant's stripes for him, but that was less in his mind than the saving of the payroll with which he had been entrusted.

They rode swiftly, needing all the distance they could get. Would Brian leave the women and follow them? He doubted it, but of all the officers in the unit, not excepting Devereaux, Brian was the man least to be trifled with.

They forded Silas Creek in a swampy area and struck a dim trail leading south across the basin. He glanced back, and saw nothing.

Dorsey was following him, some thirty feet back, and Dorsey grinned at him when he looked around, and there was something in the grin that West did not like. Yet he felt that perhaps he was finding fault where there was none. Dorsey had at least agreed to come with him.

The horses were making hard work of it, for they must be almost ten thousand feet up. He slowed to a walk, then stopped and swung down. "We'd better walk them a way," he said. "It's easy to kill a horse at this altitude."

Dorsey got down and they walked along, the trail behind them obscured by trees now. The country through which they traveled was still, cool, and beautiful. Peaks lifted before them, a thousand feet higher than they now were.

"Bear more to the right, I think," Dorsey suggested. "We're too far west for Sioux Pass."

After a while he said, "That's a lot of money we're packin'."

"Too much."

"Not if it belongs to you." Dorsey's tone was casual.

"Yes, but it doesn't."

"Ever think what you could buy with that much? Sixty thousand! A man could really have himself a time! Liquor and women . . . anything he wanted. Or he could buy himself a business some place. Be set for life."

"Well, I doubt if I'll ever have that much," West said.

"You've got it now," Dorsey replied, "or half of it."

Corporal West spoke sharply. "That's not a joking matter, Dorsey! This is government money, and we're taking it back to where it belongs."

"That may be your idea."

"It is." West's voice was crisp. He was not tempted, and he wanted no more of such talk.

Dorsey stopped. "It ain't mine, West. This here's the first chance I ever had at money like that."

West turned sharply around, for Dorsey was now right behind him. "I want no more—"

His voice broke off, for Dorsey was holding a pistol aimed just above West's belt buckle.

"You didn't really figure I was goin' to let all that money get away, did you, West?"

"Don't be a fool, Dorsey! Brian's already not far behind us. . . . You wouldn't have a chance of getting away."

"I'll worry about that."

"Dorsey . . ." West's pistol was on his belt, high on the right side, butt to the fore as was regulation. The flap was buttoned down, and he knew he could never unbutton that flap and get out his gun before Dorsey could shoot . . . but would Dorsey shoot? He didn't believe it. . . . He reached for his holster, and Dorsey shot.

74

They were in a little open place, a small meadow among the trees. West felt the sharp blow of the bullet, but no pain. "You are a foolish man," he said to Dorsey. "Now you will hang."

"First, they got to catch me," Dorsey said, and watched West's knees buckle. When he had fallen, Dorsey walked over to him and took the pistol from West's holster and thrust it into his waistband.

The echo of the shot died away, and West was muttering, but Dorsey paid no attention. He got into the saddle, gathering the reins of West's horse and the lead rope on the pack horse.

"Serves you right," Dorsey said, staring down at West.

He started off, riding fast. He had two horses now, and he could switch mounts and so make better time.

Corporal West lay sprawled on the grass, and he knew he was dying. He had been shot through the body, and by the feel the bullet must have lodged against his spine, for his legs seemed to have no feeling.

His mind was clear. He saw what a fool he had been, and with a kind of despair he realized there was small chance he would ever be found. They would think him a thief, too.

Tugging himself up by pulling on a hummock of grass, he looked slowly around. It was very still. A bee was buzzing around a blue flower. A little distance off some birds were gossiping in the top of a shrub.

With clumsy fingers he pulled a tuft of grass together and tied a few blades around it to draw attention. In the earth near it he drew an arrow showing the direction in which Dorsey had gone. He lay down then, and the shock wore off and the pain began.

He must have been unconscious for a time, for when he opened his eyes the sun had moved.

He was lying there when he heard the pound of hoofs on the earth. Suddenly a horse was looming over him, and Ten Brian was swinging down.

"Dorsey"—West got the words out clearly—"stole the money. He . . . he . . . is going to . . . Sioux Pass."

"Take it easy, West." Brian knelt beside him, lifted his head carefully and gave him a swallow from his canteen.

"I . . . I didn't mean . . . I wasn't stealing. I was—"

"I know, West. You didn't trust me, and you were taking the money back the quickest way you knew how."

The wounded man nodded. "I'm sorry. I—"

"Forget it."

"Don't . . . waste time. I . . . I am dying."

"There's not much I can do for you, Corporal. To try to move you would mean pain. You've been hit bad."

"I know."

Lieutenant Tenadore Brian stood up. He had looked upon many men dying, and knew how little there was to do now, how foolish to try, under the circumstances. The man had only minutes remaining, that was all.

"You're a good man, West. I'll tell them that. I'll report that to Major Devereaux and the Colonel. I'll tell them you died trying to save the money."

"Thanks." The word was a faint whisper.

"I'll be getting on, Corporal. And don't worry—I'll come up with Dorsey."

He stepped into the saddle, saluted the dying man, and rode away.

Corporal West lay still, looking up at the sky. The birds were fussing, and then they stopped and from somewhere across the meadow he heard a meadow lark, as he had heard them in the fields as a boy. He used to go out to bring in the cows, and the meadow larks would be there. Their song was a sound he loved to hear.

He heard it again . . . just over the way, there.

Chapter 10

The wind blew cold from off the Sweetwater Needles; from the flanks of Atlantic Peak and Granite Peak it swept over the last winter's snow through the brush, and down across the flats. It stirred the aspens along the slopes, and brought the smell of pines to Tenadore Brian.

His time was short, his pace hard. Dorsey was somewhere ahead of him, and the man would fight. He had stolen and he had committed murder, and he would know that now there was no turning back.

His horses must be just ahead. Their tracks were fresh, and Brian rode with his rifle in his hand, prepared for anything.

He wove among the pines, and rode along a grassy slope flecked with spring flowers. His horse's hoofs in their swift passing pressed down the grass and flowers, but when the horse had gone on, the grass would rise into place again, and the flowers would bloom as before.

A flicker of sunlight shone on a rifle barrel and he whipped the gray around in a tight circle, heard the *whap* of a rifle bullet that passed him, and then he was charging toward the boulders from which the shot had come.

There was no cover where he had been, it was this or

death, and he went up the short slope, reins free, the rifle ready. He heard another shot, but he was coming on fast and Dorsey was shooting too quick. He leaped the horse over the outer rim of rocks and fired twice. His first shot was a clean miss; the second hit the action of Dorsey's rifle and spun the man around. Dorsey dropped the gun and jumped at Brian, grabbing his rifle by the barrel.

Kicking free of the stirrups, Brian left the saddle in a long dive and hit Dorsey, knocking him rolling. They both came up fast, and Dorsey had Brian's rifle.

Brian flipped the gun from his holster and fired, the bullet catching Dorsey in the chest. The man backed up and Brian walked in on him, slapping the rifle from his suddenly useless hands.

"You're a murderer, Dorsey. You killed a good man back there—a better man than you ever were."

Hatred blazed in Dorsey's eyes. "You'll never get out of this, Brian! You're *trapped!*"

Dorsey sat down abruptly and the blood started to come from the hole in his chest, bubbling with a froth that told the bullet had gone through the lung.

"They're all around you, Brian! The Kelsey boys! You'll die here with me."

Ten Brian picked up the rifle and walked across to the gray. For a moment his eyes swept the area.

Dorsey's three horses stood in a hollow about twenty yards away. He noted the position of the reins and the lead rope. He ignored Dorsey. The man was finished. All he could do now was shout obscene oaths.

His eyes sweeping the brush and trees, measuring the distances, Brian reloaded his rifle and pistol. Then he walked to where Dorsey's guns had fallen and picked them up. The rifle he ignored, for it was damaged beyond repair.

He glanced at Dorsey. The man's shirt was thick with blood now, his breath was coming in great gasps,

78

but he still was half reclining against a rock, his eyes ugly.

Loading Dorsey's guns, Brian thrust them both into his own waistband. Taking his own horse by the bridle, he led it down into the hollow. He gathered the reins of the others, tied them for leading, and then walked to the edge of the hollow.

He disliked leaving even an enemy to suffer as Dorsey would be suffering, but there was nothing he could do, and his duty was to Mary Devereaux and Belle Renick. When Dorsey chose to kill Corporal West he had invited death to himself. He had gambled and he had lost.

Ten Brian stood and looked out across the country to the north. He did not know that Kelsey and his men, or some of his men, were out there, but he had a feeling they were. Probably they were behind him, moving up even now. Yet they might be out there in front. That was a gamble he had to take.

On foot, leading the horses and keeping himself between two of them, he went out of the hollow into the larger basin of the Little Popo Agie. He paused, seeming to look around him as though looking for a place to picket his horses. He went around a small hill, and quickly stepped into the saddle. He went out the other side at a trot, swung around a clump of trees, and broke into a run.

Behind him there was a shot ... fired from too far away at a moving target, it did not even come close. He ran his horses for half a mile, then proceeded to weave an intricate trail through the trees. He doubled back, then followed a creek for a few hundred yards, and emerging, went scrambling up a small slide of rock and into the trees again. When he had ridden a little further he changed over to West's horse to give his own some needed rest.

They were behind him and they would keep coming. They might choose not to bother with a trail but to

79

head directly for Sweetwater Gap . . . if they knew of it.

The sun went down in a wilderness of color, brilliant at this high altitude. Then shadows came among these high peaks, and night came on.

He pushed on until he had crossed the Roaring Fork once more. There he moved up under the trees, stripped the gear from the horses and picketed them on a small meadow far enough back from the stream so he could hear any approach. He searched through the saddlebags and came on some jerky and hardtack. He ate, and then bringing the gray in closer to him, he slept.

Daylight had not come when he awoke. He saddled the gray first, then the other horses. Dorsey's horse was bigger, and he put the packs on it.

Mounting up then, he started off. Two hours later he saw them, saddled up and ready to move out. They had camped in another little area of pothole lakes.

Mary ran a few steps and stopped, waiting for him to come up. "Ten! Oh, Ten, I was so afraid!"

"What happened?"

"I mean . . . for you."

The others came to him as he swung down. His face was haggard from the lack of sleep and the hard riding. "I caught up . . . Dorsey killed West and took the money. West wasn't quite dead when I found him . . . I came up to Dorsey a little later. He missed and I didn't."

"He *shot* at you?" Belle exclaimed.

"That was a lot of money he had. I guess he was already spending it."

"There's coffee on," Mary said. "You must take some time."

He drank it, feeling the warmth steal through him. He looked up at the mountains towering hundreds of feet on either side. They were almost at the mouth of the gap, and he could see where the mountains closed in.

"We'd better walk," he said, "and save our horses for later." He turned toward Ironhide. "Did you go up and look around?"

"No . . . only I think there is snow."

Brian could almost taste it on the wind. And even when they were through the gap they would not be free, for Kelsey would be between them and the safety of Fort Bridger.

He felt the weight of the pistol on his hip as he looked at the gathering clouds. A storm at this altitude could be dangerous. He had witnessed some frightening electrical storms among mountain peaks before this.

"They're coming up behind me, I think," he said, "but we can not overlook the possibility that they may be at the other side of the pass. It depends on how much they know of these mountains. All I know of these passes is hearsay."

He took his time with the coffee, chewed on a piece of jerky, and dipped some hardtack in the coffee to soften it.

"Ironhide," he said, looking up, "you take the pack horses and lead off. The girls will come behind you, then Schwartz. I'm going to finish my coffee, and then I'll catch up."

"Do you mind if I wait and ride with you?" Mary asked.

"I'd like that," he said.

Before he moved out of camp he emptied the pot on the fire. He pulled the partly burned pieces of wood from the fire and crushed the charred ends to kill any possible sparks, then threw dirt over what remained.

"You are careful," Mary said.

"I've seen what fire can do," he said. "I've seen thousands of acres burned off for no good reason, and it takes years to replace—if it is ever replaced."

Mounting up, they started into the pass together. The

air was cold and crisp. The clouds had moved in, shrouding the peaks with cottony gray. In the distance, thunder rumbled.

There was no sound in the pass but the sound of hoofs and the creak of saddles, and a slight stir of wind. Here and there were patches of snow, some of them fairly deep.

They rode side by side without talking, but listening for any other sound that might come to them. The pass was something over three miles long; they caught up with the others where Ironhide had stopped to let the horses get their breath. They had been living at an altitude of slightly over four thousand feet, and the change to nearly ten thousand feet made them short of breath and unable to do hard traveling for extended periods.

Ahead of them a slide had piled a great mass of snow across the pass. Ironhide had walked upon the great drift, and found the surface was hard, probably hard enough to bear the weight of a horse.

Leading their horses, they slipped and scrambled across, one at a time. A little way ahead they saw another snow slide, and a jumble of boulders. Brian was helping the last horse across the second slide when Schwartz came up to him. He had climbed up the steep slide to get a good view back down the pass.

"They're after us, sir," he said. "There's about a dozen of them."

"How far back?"

"I was using Miss Devereaux's glasses, sir. I could just make them out. I'd say they are about where we camped last night."

The pass had become narrower, and the wind was stronger, but the clouds were lower. The rumble of thunder sounded close by. But it would be safer right in the pass than out of it, for the lightning would almost certainly be drawn to the higher rocks.

They moved ahead, though slowly. There was no

question of hurry. Neither horses nor men were up to it. Brian and Ironhide felt it least. They were almost at the highest point of the pass now, when before them appeared a massive wall of tumbled boulders and a huge slide that blocked the pass completely.

Schwartz stared up at it, his face pale. "We'll not get cross that one, sir. It's impossible."

Ten Brian studied the slide, and the mountain on both sides. Such slides as these were gradually wearing down the steep slopes and cliffs, and some time in the future the pass would be less difficult, but now there was no way of taking a horse up the steep walls of the pass. He walked over to the snow slide.

The wall of snow was at least thirty feet high, slopping steeply up. He reached back to his scabbard and brought out his bowie knife. Tentatively, he cut into the snow. It was a more recent slide, and somewhat less icy than the others. It cut easily, and in a few moments he had cut out a fair-sized block.

Schwartz had come up to him, holding a shovel. "When we left the ambulance, sir, I tied this on the pack horse. I figured we might need it."

"Good man. We'll try cutting some steps."

It was tiring work, and the three men took turns digging into the snow with the shovel or bowie knife, cutting steps easy enough for the horses. In some places the snow was softer, and would be difficult to cross over.

Mary called to Brian, "The men who are coming will have it easier. They won't have to do all this digging."

"We'll see about that. Ironhide, take your horse and try it."

The Cherokee led his horse forward. The animal balked, but urged on, it finally took a tentative step, them scrambled up and up. Soon it disappeared from view.

"All right, Belle," Brian said.

They waited as she went, and her horse made it up without trouble.

"Schwartz, get them over and get my horse over," Brian said then. He had taken up his Henry rifle.

"You can't stop them. Not one man, sir."

"I don't plan to . . . but I will make them a bit more cautious."

He climbed up on the slide behind them, settled down behind a log and lowered his rifle into a forked limb. He looked back. The men behind were perhaps a mile away, and coming on. As they drew nearer he took careful aim at one of the men and fired.

The shot reverberated down the pass in echoes. He could not see the bullet strike, but the man at whom he had fired jumped back and fell. A moment later he got up. The others had stopped.

Coolly, Brian fired three more shots, and the men disappeared from view. He had hit nothing, he was sure, but he had put the bullets in their area and it would slow them up a little, which was all he had hoped to accomplish. He got down off the snow; the others had disappeared over the slide.

He knew that his shots would make the Kelsey men cautious, for they would be wary of a man who would attempt a shot at such a distance and come so close; but Ten Brian had aided in the testing of rifles, calculating trajectories and patterns.

He climbed the steps cut into the slide ahead. They were ragged steps now, for the horses had sprawled a good deal, occasionally breaking through icy crust. He made it to the top and looked over.

Before him lay the Sweetwater River which began in the mountains on his right. The pass before him was green, with only spots of snow remaining. The stream was ruffling over the rocks, and even a few wild flowers were showing . . . but there was nothing else.

Not a horse, not a person. The pass before him was empty; as far as he could see there was nothing.

Not even his own horse. . . .

84

Chapter 11

There had been no shots. In the narrow pass he could not have missed hearing them.

His party might have gone on down the pass to find shelter before the coming rain. That seemed the only logical answer, and the simplest explanation is usually the one to accept . . . unless your life depends on it.

They might have run into a party of Indians, but the likely explanation was that Kelsey had foreseen their emergence from this pass and had men waiting for them here.

He had forty men, it was said. He could easily detach five men for this pass and five for Sioux Pass without crippling his force too much. And if he had men waiting here for the others, and had taken them, he would be expecting Brian also. It was possible he had one or two men waiting down there with rifles. Under the circumstances, Reuben Kelsey would prefer a dead Brian to a live one.

Drawing back from the crest of the slide, he worked his way along it to the east wall of the pass. Here he could go up the side of the mountain under cover of the aspens.

When he had climbed at least two hundred feet he turned to look back.

The great slide was behind him now, for he had

angled across the face of the mountain in making the climb. There was timber in the pass, but also there were open places that were green. He could see a faint trail in the grass left by riders coming out of the pass and disappearing into the trees.

Crouching on his heels, he peered through the stand of aspen and tried to make out what lay below and ahead of him. After a while, moving on cat feet, he worked his way along the slope. He had gone only a short distance when, glancing down through the trees, he saw a man crouching behind some rocks. He held a rifle in his hand and he was watching the slide.

For a moment Brian considered attempting to go down the slope to the man, but he would almost certainly be heard, and because of the intervening growth, a bullet might be deflected. He pulled back and continued silently along the slope. For some time, perhaps for an hour, the man would stay there. Suddenly he thought . . . a horse! Somewhere nearby the man's horse must be picketed.

Ever so slowly, and working with infinite care, he eased down the slope, searching from every vantage point for a glimpse of the horse.

And then he saw him, feeding in a small meadow some two hundred yards from the hidden rifleman.

It took him twenty minutes of painstaking work to get to the horse, but only seconds to gather the reins and get into the saddle. Yet at this moment a horse was not what he wanted, for any rider would be under observation by the Kelsey outfit wherever they were. Searching for an opening, he found one, and scrambled the horse up the slope into the trees.

For several minutes he stayed in the saddle, working his way along the slope, pausing every time he could get a glimpse of the pass below or the opening valley ahead. He could still see the trail in the grass, and could see it as well from up on the mountainside as in the valley. Only now he could see two trails, one evidently made when Kelsey's riders came up the valley.

He was now on the flank of Atlantic Peak, with the Sweetwater Needles ahead. Most of the peak was above timberline, so he kept lower, working his way around deadfalls and blow-downs.

Suddenly he saw the horse's ears prick and he drew up. Down through the trees, off the slope and on the very edge of a wide sweep of grassland he saw a camp, almost a mile away. Smoke was lifting from a fire and he could see movement. He rode on, carefully working his way closer. He was several hundred feet higher than the camp, and when he decided he was within a quarter of a mile he drew up and got down.

For the first time he checked the saddle. There was an empty rifle scabbard, a blanket roll behind the saddle, a pair of saddlebags.

He opened one of these and found a small sack of .44's, caps, and two loaded cylinders. A neatly wrapped packet of jerky and hardtack, and in the very bottom a dozen rings, several watches, and a handful of coins, mostly gold. It was obviously loot from the wagon train.

In the other saddlebag there was a pair of socks, a sack of tobacco, and a derringer, double barreled and loaded. He pocketed the .44's and the spare cylinders, the packet of food, and the derringer. Then with his knife he cut the saddle strings from the saddle, and stuffing the other items into a pocket, he took one string and fastened a lanyard to which he tied the trigger guard of the derringer. Slipping off his coat, he tied the rawhide around his arm above the elbow to let the gun dangle within two inches of the edge of his cuff. Then he put on his coat.

Leaving the horse tied to some brush he went on along the slope, always moving carefully. When closer to the camp he squatted down among the aspen and studied the layout.

Judging by the horses, there were at least ten men

87

down below. Some were sprawled on the ground sleeping; one was cleaning a rifle, another was preparing food over a fire, and others were idling about, talking. He could hear no voices, and he worked his way down the slope, wary of making the slightest sound. When he stopped again he could distinguish the voices, and he could also see his gray horse, and several other horses he thought he recognized.

Shifting his position so he could see further to the right, he glimpsed Mary and Belle. Both were seated on the ground; both apparently had their wrists and ankles tied. Near them was Schwartz, and further away, Ironhide. Thoughtfully, Brian studied the layout of the camp. He could now make out scattered bits of conversation.

Finally one of the men said explosively, "Damn it! Where's Reub? I want to get this business over!"

"Take it easy, Hob. He'll be along. You know how he is, an' if he ain't here, he's got a reason."

So they were waiting for Kelsey. When he arrived he would likely have more of the renegades with him and Brian's chances would be less. If he were to do anything it must be done quickly. His idea of waiting for darkness would not work. Thunder rumbled among the peaks. He glanced up at Atlantic and saw that the summit was banked with black clouds. A few spatters of rain fell, and then the rain came with a rush.

Getting up, Brian walked back to the horse and broke open the bedroll. As he had expected, the slicker was there. "A fair weather rider," he muttered, "to pack his slicker." He put on the slicker, then rolled the blankets and put them on behind the saddle.

The prisoners were huddled under a spreading tree, and their captors were now putting a lean-to together. Brian glanced down at the slicker he wore, and then without a moment's hesitation, he turned back, and found a way down the slope. He held his rifle under the slicker in his right hand. When he reached the bottom the rain was like a gray curtain. He came out of the brush near the camp, walked directly up to where the women and soldiers waited under the tree.

Slipping his knife from its scabbard, he thrust it down behind the ropes that bound Ironhide's wrists. They were snug, but the blade had an edge like a razor. The ropes cut through, he turned quickly to Mary.

He had cut her ropes and had turned to Schwartz while Ironhide was freeing Belle, when a man came up. "Joe," he said, "did you get that lieutenant? We never heard no shot."

Brian merely grunted and the man came closer. "Look," he said, "if you came back without—"

His eyes widened and he started to yell, but Brian jammed the muzzle of the rifle into his wind, then swung a short, chopping stroke with the butt, using both hands. The man grunted and fell over.

"Up the slope!" Brian said. "There's one horse up there."

Turning, he started toward the line of horses, walking swiftly. The men were clustered around the shelter. Suddenly one of them turned, saw the prisoners gone, and started to shout just as Brian reached the horses. He cut the rope to which they were tied, and grabbed the bridle on his gray, swinging the horse around. Nobody had bothered to take the weapons from the saddles of the captured men, and he caught up the bridles and started to move.

The man who had seen the prisoners gone, spun around, yelling as he grabbed for a gun. Brian had slammed his rifle down into the boot and had whipped up his six-gun.

Putting the spurs to the gray, he fired three times into the crowd around the lean-to, even as his horse was pounding toward the man who had yelled. The man had his gun swinging up when the gray's shoulder hit him and knocked him spinning. Brian fired down at him, knew he had missed, and turned in the saddle to let go with another shot at the crowd around the lean-to.

He was past the place where he had come down the slope, but he turned the gray up the hill in a pounding scramble, the other horses coming behind.

He was scarcely at the spot where the other horse waited when Ironhide leaped from the brush into the saddle. Schwartz hurried the horses to the women. Mary was already upon the captured horse, but they were one short. Schwartz caught Belle in his arms and threw her into the saddle, then got up behind her and they went along the slope, wet branches slapping at their faces.

Beyond the camp a trail seemed to appear from nowhere and two horses were running along it, stirrups slapping their sides. Ironhide caught one of them and Schwartz switched horses without even slowing down.

An avenue through the trees opened up and in the pounding rain they went up the mountain toward the low gray clouds.

Brian topped out on a bench almost at timberline. There was a flash of lightning that seemed like the light of a thousand bombs bursting at once, then a shattering roar of thunder. The others came up behind him, their faces weirdly lit by a more distant flash, and then he was leading off around the mountain, running the big gray.

He turned a shoulder of the mountain and started east, skirting the pines, dipped down into a hollow, and slowed the gray to let the others catch up. He was the only one wearing a slicker, the only one with any kind of protection.

None of the gear had been removed from the horses in the short space of time after their arrival at the camp, and now, waiting in the hollow, Mary dug into her pack for a raincoat, and Belle did the same. Ironhide cut a hole in the blanket from the captured horse and put his head through it.

There was no trail for them here. A dim game trail showed along the mountain, but such trails are often made by animals that can go under low-hanging boughs, and they cannot always be trusted. Yet it pointed a way, and they took it, anxious to get off the summit where lightning might strike at any time.

Down the game trail they went, through a maze of boulders fallen from a shattered cliff, around a bulging rock, and into a scattering of trees with many blow-downs.

Brian pulled up alongside Ironhide. "We've got to find some shelter—a cave or something."

The Cherokee nodded. He had been looking for something of the sort.

Through the slanting rain they saw a vast sweep of open country, a plain reaching away to lose itself in the gray rain and the gathering night.

Only moments were left to them. He was looking for something—a space between fallen slabs, a natural shelter created by blown-down trees ... anything that would suffice.

Mary caught his arm. "There!"

It was up the slope, a tiny cleft of blackness against the rain-wet rock. He turned in his saddle. "No use all of us going up. I'll have a look."

The gray took the slope easily, and against the face of the rock he found what seemed like an ancient trail. It was a hopeful sign.

He was almost to the spot before he drew up in disappointment. It was not a break in the rock, but a pine tree growing there close against the face, with no other pines close by. When he started to turn there was not room enough and he went on to the tree, and turned there. He had swung the gray and cast one last quick look around, when he saw the opening of a cave that had been hidden by the tree.

He rode down a slight slope to the entrance, which was all of thirty feet wide and not over eight feet high at the highest. It was a cave, and it was shelter. He turned back and motioned the others on, but they could scarcely see him, so he rode back and led them to the cave.

It was dry inside, and was about fifty feet deep, although at one time it might have been much deeper. Now it was blocked off by a rock-fall.

He gathered sticks from the debris around the entrance and broke the smaller lower limbs, all dead, from the pine, and kindled a fire. There was a good-sized shelf before the cave, close to the pine, and there they let the horses graze, after stripping the gear from them.

The fire blazed up, crackling cheerfully. Mary held her hands out to it, and looked up at Ten, smiling. "It takes very little to make one comfortable, after all," she said.

He nodded. "But when you have it, there's nothing like it. A little shelter, a little fire . . . a little food, a corner away from the wind. Sometimes I think the further a man gets from the simple basic needs the less happy he is. Out there is the storm, and beyond the storm, enemies . . . but there is nothing that seems as good as this when you need it."

Ironhide came in and squatted near the fire, feeding the flames with small sticks. The light played strangely on his dark features, but when he looked over the fire at them he smiled. "I guess a man doesn't have to be an Indian to like this," he said.

Outside the rain poured down, thunder continued to roll. They made beds from the blanket rolls, and whatever else they could use, and bedded down in the cave. Lying there in her wet garments, the heat slowly warming the dampness away, Mary Devereaux looked out at the blackness of the night. Occasionally a distant flash of lightning showed the pines and the rocks in a ragged edge against the night, but close by was the welcome fire.

Mary felt wide awake now, and Brian felt like talking.

"I wonder if dinosaurs were ever in this cave?" Mary said.

"I doubt if the cave was even here in the dinosaur days. Or these mountains, for that matter. I think these mountains were late in developing. But mountains were here, I think. Mountains that were worn away by wind and rain and time, and then other mountains. It still goes on. This storm will make changes, most of them very small. But seeds fall into cracks and plants grow up to spread the cracks wider with their roots. Rain washes in, snow melts, the winter freezes, and the cracks in the rocks expand.

"There's no end to it, and here we can see it happening. There's a majesty in it, a timeless sort of beauty. I love to see some of the gnarled old trees; cedars and bristle-cone pines are favorites of mine, for so often they live where it doesn't seem possible to live. They grow right out of rocks, gnarled and twisted and old . . . but strong, stronger than anything but time, and they are part of time.

Brian paused. "Men make too much of their problems," he went on. "So many things grow small and petty when you see them through the window of time. I started out when I was a youngster, and sometimes it seems as if I've lived two or three lives; and I see the youngsters now excited about the same things, all wanting to change the world overnight, when it never changes that way—well, not often. And when it does change that way it changes with fire and blood, and it goes back further into what we're trying to grow out of.

"I think we all should go to the mountains more often. We should stand alone and look on the peaks and the valleys. . . . Have you ever seen the Tetons? Or looked over the wide, unending plains?"

Brian paused. "Well, I've rambled along and put

Belle and Schwartz to sleep. Now I'd better let you sleep. We'll need all the rest we can get."

"Will we leave first thing in the morning?" Mary asked.

He shrugged. "We might stay right here. If we don't make any tracks they surely can't find any. The trouble is, we didn't get the gold. And I've got that to do."

He went out into the rain and gathered more fuel. He broke off larger limbs from the blow-downs and dragged them back, placing them close to the fire where he could reach out of his blankets and put a fresh stick on the fire. Then he bedded down and lay wide awake for a while, with the smell of rain and a wood fire around him, and the realization that Mary was here, close by.

She probably didn't give a thought to him, and why should she? A drifter, a ne'er-do-well, a soldier who fought for anybody who had a war, and who after thirty rough years had no more future than a spent bullet.

When they used to tell him that a rolling stone gathered no moss, he always replied that it did get a smooth polish ... and that a wandering bee got the honey. Well, he had the polish, he supposed, and here and there he'd had a taste of the honey, but right now the taste in his mouth was a bitter one.

He closed his eyes and tried to shut out his thoughts. It would be better just to listen to the rain falling, to smell the pines and the wood smoke. They couldn't take that from him—the memory of countless lonely fires built in countless lonely places, a memory that leaves a man with a taste for wild country.

At last he fell asleep, and he did not awaken when Ironhide got up and slipped out into the night. The rain was slackening, and the Cherokee, after a glance back into the cave, disappeared in the darkness.

Chapter 12

When Lieutenant Tenadore Brian awoke suddenly some hours later, it was not yet dawn, but his senses told him the hour was not far away. He lay still and considered the situation. He believed their wild ride through the night had left pursuit far behind, and the rain must have washed away whatever tracks they had made.

The cave in such an out-of-the-way spot was not likely to be known to the Kelsey men, nor easily found by them. They had some food, though not much, and Brian decided his idea of the night before was a good one—to remain right where they were, making no tracks whatsoever.

And then he began to think about the gold.

When he had ordered the army ambulance away from the wagon train, taking over command without authorization, he had assumed responsibility for the payroll as well as for the women, and therefore it was up to him to recover the gold.

In studying the problem, Reuben Kelsey had to be considered first, and what did he know of him?

Little enough, though years ago they had for several weeks moved across the country together. At that time Kelsey was sixteen and it might be assumed that his character was formed to a considerable degree.

He was a reckless boy, tall and handsome, unusually powerful, perfectly coordinated, and already a good woodsman. He had lived in Missouri and Texas, had fought Comanches at fourteen, Kiowas at fifteen, and shortly before the wagon train started west he had killed a bad man from east Texas in a hand-to-hand fight.

He was a natural leader, ready to put himself forward, and gifted with a strong vein of caution for all his seeming recklessness. He and Brian had become friends from necessity, But Ten Brian in those days had been a quiet boy, retiring, and with a preference for going it alone. When with others he had usually allowed them to take the lead. He had been, he felt, as good a woodsman as Kelsey, but Kelsey assumed that Brian was not up to his own capabilities; and Brian, knowing they would get along better as long as Kelsey had that idea, did nothing to change it.

Kelsey showed himself even then to be ruthless and without scruples, but he was also outwardly friendly, quick to laugh or smile—superficially a good companion.

Ten knew that Kelsey had always regarded him with amused contempt, but during the months after their escape and before Brian left for the East and the years of soldiering abroad, they had continued to be friendly. During that period Kelsey had several times told Brian that he was the only friend he had.

Since that time their paths had taken different directions. Kelsey had stayed in the West. He had trapped fur in Montana and Wyoming, had roamed the Colorado mountains, and had gone on to California, returning eventually to Missouri.

Brian's experience had been utterly different. At a time when many men were drifting from place to place, seeking their fortunes in the far-off corners of the world, he had served with the Foreign Legion in Africa.

Those were days of little rest for him. One campaign followed another, and for seven years, as enlisted man and officer, he had fought in the Atlas Mountains, and raided deep into the Tibesti region. One campaign had been fought in the Hoggar Mountains, another in the Tamanrasset. He had dealt with the Arabs, who have a saying, *kiss the hand you can not cut off,* and he had learned to be friendly but not trusting.

After that there had been Rome, and the Papal Zouaves. He had lived a year of pomp and ceremony, and then had gone off to China. Here his success in the service of the Manchu government had been rapid. He acquired the scar on his cheek in a fierce fight with bandits who attempted to rob him when he had ridden out ahead of his command. . . .

All that was long ago and far away. Now he was once more in the land he preferred to all others, and Reuben Kelsey was here . . . his enemy.

Leaning over, he took a stick and stirred the remains of the fire, then added more fuel. Belle Renick turned restlessly in her sleep, murmuring something. Outside the rain had begun again.

Sitting up, Brian tugged on his boots and stood up. It was only then that he noticed the empty bed . . . the Cherokee was gone!

For a moment he stood still, thinking. Then he took up his hat and his slicker, and reached for his rifle. Leaning over, he touched Schwartz, who was fully awake at once.

"Ironhide's gone," Brian said. "I'm going to have a look around. Stay inside and keep alert."

He went to the cave entrance and looked out. Before him lay a canyon, deep and narrow, and spiked with jutting crags and tumbled slabs of rock. Everywhere were the trunks of trees left from an old blow-down. New growth had sprung up, shrouding it all with green. From far below came the subdued sound of a rushing

97

stream. Above, the mountains were still shrouded in clouds. A light rain fell steadily.

The Cherokee had left on foot, for no horse was gone. And no tracks remained, so he had left not later than the middle of the night.

Where would he go? To Major Devereaux, for help? He would have taken a horse for that. Or back to the Kelsey outfit after the gold?

Brian went outside the cave, and from the shelter of the towering pine he let his eyes rove over the area about them.

Mary had come up beside him. "Where do you think he's gone?" she said.

"He's gone after the payroll. That's all it could be, and that means I've got to go after him. He may need help."

She was silent for a moment. "I don't want you to go, Ten," she said then, "but I know you must."

"I have to. You'll be safe here, I think—safer than trying to get away."

He was studying the mountain. It would be easier to go over the shoulder than around it, as they had come. He could keep under cover part of the way, and much of the part above timberline was invisible from below.

The Cherokee was a good Indian. He would be hard to trap, but he might be too confident. Reuben Kelsey would be out there now, furious at their escape. Of course, he might just take the money and leave; but that opened another line of thought ... sixty thousand was a lot of money. It was unlikely the group would ever make as big a strike again, and Kelsey would realize that. Wasn't it likely that he would try to get it all for himself? That meant he must get away somehow, with the gold, and without pursuit.

"Listen," he said to Mary. "If I am not back in two days, leave this place, and when you start, stay up on the mountain as long as you can."

She looked at him intently, her eyes serious. He

98

wondered how many times she had seen her father ride away on patrols into Indian country, never sure if she would see him again. That was why she stood so still now, concealing whatever she felt, knowing he had to go, and wasting no time in pleading or protest.

He would leave his horse. The gray needed the rest, and if he needed a horse he would use one of theirs; for if he got in position to save Ironhide or the gold he would also be in a position to take a horse.

"Take care," he said gently, and bent swiftly and kissed her on the cheek, squeezing her arm slightly. Wheeling, he crossed the small clearing and went up the slope into the trees, dripping with rain.

Mary stood alone, looking after him, then turned abruptly and went back into the cave.

Belle was standing there. "Now you have two of them to worry about. It never gets any easier, Mary. Take it from me, who has had twenty years of saying good-bye."

"He'll be back."

"Yes, I think so. He's the kind who will come back if anybody does. He has a gift for survival."

Mary looked up the slope again. There was nothing to show that a man had passed that way.

"Are you in love with him, Mary?" Belle asked.

"Yes, I believe I am."

Schwartz stood by them. "He's a good man," he said, "a good man and a good officer. He thinks of his men always."

Mary sat down by the fire and fed small sticks into it.

Up on the slope Ten Brian moved along under the trees. He liked the woods, and he liked them in a rain. Two or three times he stopped, standing very still and listening to the forest sounds, letting his ears grow accustomed to the sound of the rain, and all the while being alert for any other sounds. But he kept moving ahead steadily and quietly.

There might be men out searching for them, and he might encounter them at any time, but he had serious doubts that the outlaws would undergo the discomfort of the woods at such a time.

When he had crossed the ridge by a devious route, he came at last to a place above the camp of the renegades where he could look down on it. He was some distance above the camp, and he studied it from a sheltered position under a tree that had partly fallen and lodged in the branches of another one. Other debris had collected among the fallen tree's branches until it had formed a sort of roof, sufficient for a man to hide under, or even for a man and a horse.

The view down the mountain was good, but up the mountain it was masked by close-growing trees, blow-downs, and rocks. He could make out a steep and very narrow trail, weaving among the rocks and trees. It had probably been used by Indians and by game, but where it went Brian could not guess.

Looking down, he could see that some of the rene-gades' horses, recaptured, were tied to trees near the camp. There was no person in sight. Was Ironhide a prisoner there, or was he lurking in some such hiding place as Brian had found? His own position here was perfect, except that he would not be able to get down the mountain easily, but would have to go round about. Sheltered from view as well as from wind and rain, he sat on a log and watched. After a while a man came out from the lean-to, gathered some fuel, and went back inside.

Suddenly there was a pound of hoofs and a party of four horsemen came up, dismounted and walked up to the lean-to, which had grown in size with added work. Brian stood up, craning his neck for a better view. He saw that one of the riders was Reuben Kelsey!

The man must weigh two hundred and fifty pounds, and was broad and powerful. He wore a buckskin jacket, fringed, and the muscles of his shoulders and arms made the material bulge. He had a heavy shock of almost blonde hair and a mustache. Big as he was, he moved with ease and grace, stepping lightly. The men behind him were an oddly assorted crew, but they looked like tough customers. All of them disappeared inside. He had no desire to make contact with the renegades if it could be avoided. What he wanted was to get the payroll back, and he wanted Ironhide safe. His problem now was to find out where they both were, and what Kelsey intended to do.

It had been years since he had known Kelsey, but he doubted if the man's character had changed much. He had been a bold, daring boy, gifted with animal cunning, a ferocious fighter with fists or any kind of weapon. Brian's first conclusion was, he was positive, the correct one. Reuben Kelsey would try to get all the sixty thousand dollars for himself. That would mean he had first had to get rid of most of the men, get them off on a chase or by some sort of excuse. Then he had to get the money away from the others and ride out of the country.

West was the most likely direction. East would take him in the direction of Fort Laramie, of Julesburg, just the places he would be recognized by the renegades or their friends. West, but not directly; it would be northwest. He would try for the mines in Montana, for Virginia City, or—?

But why? Kelsey did not need more money; he would want to spend what he had, and that meant San Francisco or the East. East meant through Blackfoot country, or the edge of it through Sioux country, where army patrols might be encountered.

San Francisco then, but by the Oregon Trail to the coast.

And yet, even as Brian decided that was what Reuben Kelsey would do, he felt a stir of doubt. He could remember Reuben . . . he had always been devious, likely to do the unexpected.

101

First things first. Undoubtedly some of the men were hunting Ten Brian and the women, or would be soon, and Kelsey would find some way to get rid of the others.

Brian sat still, studying the layout anew. There seemed to be no way of approaching the lean-to without being seen, and now, since the women were freed, the renegades would be doubly on guard.

Again Kelsey came outside, and he stood there in the open, looking around. He stretched, then turned casually and looked up at the mountain.

Instinctively, Brian drew back, then cursed himself for a fool. There was no chance that he could be seen, hidden as he was, but from Kelsey's manner he would have sworn the man knew that he was there.

Not only was he sure that Kelsey was aware of his presence; more than that, he felt that Kelsey was glad that he was there!

Chapter 13

In the valley of the Sweetwater, Major Devereaux sat under the canvas shelter and worked on the report he must send back to the Fort. Thus far he had seen no evidence of hostiles, but he had met and fought a brief skirmish with renegades led by Reuben Kelsey. This would be important information, and it changed the status of things somewhat.

Kelsey was not a man to be taken lightly, nor was his presence on the Overland Trail. Rounding him up was a matter of the greatest importance. So was the recovery of the payroll, to say nothing of his own daughter and the wife of Captain Renick.

At this point he was without information. His hunters had killed two buffalo, several antelope, and one deer. Now the men were eating, and at the moment resting.

Four scouts were out, working in two pairs. One pair had ridden into the mountains to the east of Granite Peak; the other two men had been scouting the plains to the south and west.

Lieutenant Cahill, with a patrol of ten men, was scouting to the north. Cahill was a competent officer, but he had completely lost touch with Kelsey's band. After the brief skirmish in the valley of the Beaver they had vanished like smoke.

Kelsey's men were woodsmen, hardly inferior, many of them, to the Carson type of mountain man, and when they wanted to vanish, they did so simply and effectively. The band had, like Indians, scattered in as many directions as there were men. There was not one trail, there were forty or more. They crisscrossed and circled, and merged with old trails or new. They fell in with the tracks of Devereaux's own command; then they were gone, and somehow there was nothing.

Cahill, who had served much of his frontier time in the states along the Mexican border, found it different here. There pursuit was simpler, even if difficult. There the Apache could make his trail hard to find, but the Indian needed waterholes; and with knowledge of waterholes one stood a chance, at least.

Here, there was water everywhere. The trees hid movement, the canyons offered ready places of concealment, and hiding was no longer a problem. But sooner or later they must move, and in moving they must leave a trail.

Cahill scouted the country with care and caution. He knew the manner of men they faced, and knew that there was small chance of trapping them. Yet there was a chance that they might come upon them suddenly, or catch them in camp.

He nooned in Omena Meadow near Beaver Creek, then skirted Limestone Mountain to the head of Pass Creek. He found many tracks, and Turpenning said all were made by Kelsey's men, apparently in seeking for Brian and his party.

Cahill could go little further with the time allowed, and he called Turpenning again. "Take Webster and ride north," he said; "scout the country and join us at the head of Sioux Pass."

When Turpenning had gone he moved the patrol west, scattering his men to look for sign, and approaching the pass in a wide-flung skirmish line.

They found nothing. Resting at the head of Sioux Pass he was joined by Turpenning.

"He's got a spare horse, sir," Turpenning said, "and somebody or something over the saddle." What he had found were the bodies of West and Dorsey.

Turpenning squatted on his heels alongside the fire. "Sign reads plain enough. West and Dorsey rode together with a packhoss. Looks as if West had the payroll and was started back. Then Dorsey evidently shot him . . . leastways that's the way it reads.

"Brian—that big gray of his is easy to spot—found West, then he went after Dorsey and fetched up with him. Dorsey came out the short end of the horn. Brian went off to the north with the packhoss."

"We'll bury them here," Devereaux said and he detailed a burial party, then went back to Turpenning, who sat by the fire. For a moment Cahill stared into the flames. He knew that such men as Turpenning, who were skilled trackers, often read more from intuition than from what sign there was.

"What do you think, Turp?" he asked.

The Tennessean hesitated, then shrugged. "Kelsey would know about the passes. He would have men watching them. Sure as shootin' he'll be waitin' when Lieutenant Brian comes out of the mountains—an' he's got to come out. He hasn't much grub along, an' he has two women with him, an' just two men left. He'll come out of those hills at one of the passes north of here . . . Sweetwater Gap, most likely. A man doesn't have all that much choice. And he'll run into Kelsey.

"From there you got to guess. It depends on who sees who first, and what kind of a spot they're in when it happens. Brian's goin' to have to be cunnin'. He can't outrun them. The Kelsey outfit have some of the best horseflesh I ever seen, and there's a-plenty of them. He's got two things Kelsey wants. The women and the money."

Cahill considered a moment, and then called another

trooper. He scratched out a brief message to Major Devereaux.

Found bodies of West and Dorsey. Proceeding through Sioux Pass. Will camp on Little Sweetwater near point of trees.

Cahill

There were tracks in Sioux Pass, the tracks of strange horses . . . Kelsey men, for the tracks were fresh.

Cahill and his patrol made camp in the point of trees near the Little Sweetwater in a driving rain. Hastily they threw up shelters and built fires under cover of the trees. At that moment they were less than ten miles from the cave that sheltered Mary Devereaux and the others.

Cahill walked out in the rain and stood under the last of the trees with Webster. "After they eat I'll send two men out, Web, but keep a sharp eye out. They'll come south, I am sure of that, and they will hold close to the edge of the mountains."

"I think so, sir."

Cahill looked again into the slanting rain. Brian was out there somewhere with two men and two women and the payroll.

"I hope he makes out, sir."

Cahill nodded. "I do, too. If anyone can, he can."

"I know Kelsey, sir. He's a devil. He raided my brother's farm back in the Ozarks. Stripped it, and then turned in his saddle and shot my brother. With his wife looking on. He was doing nothing . . . just standing."

"I've heard such things about him."

He walked back to the fires, shivering as he extended his hands to the warmth. He could smell the buffalo meat broiling over the flames.

Ten Brian went down the mountain by a roundabout route and scouted the camp. Only eight men remained in camp, with Kelsey himself. There were ten horses, which meant that either two men were on guard somewhere near, or the spare horses were pack horses, one for the gold, the other for supplies.

The rain still fell, and Ten studied the layout, trying to guess where the gold might be. To attempt to take it from so many men was out of the question. He would have the problem of escape.

And *where was Ironhide?*

As he watched, Reuben Kelsey emerged from the lean-to carrying a saddle. The rain had eased a little, and he took his time walking to the horses, picketed only a few yards from where Ten Brian crouched in the brush near a pine tree. He wiped water from the back of a big black horse, and then adjusted the blanket.

"I'd like to talk to Ten Brian," he said in a casual, offhand tone of voice, just loud enough for Brian to hear. "Be a mighty nice thing if he was around, and within hearin'."

He stooped and picked up the saddle, and then he added, "We could make us a deal."

He tightened the girth, and stood for a moment with his hands on the saddle. "Mighty nice in San Francisco about now. A place to be. Lots of women there, a man could take his pick . . . if he had money, that is. And we could have money, the two of us."

Brian waited, listening. Was Kelsey so sure that he was within hearing? Was he really making him an offer, or was it a trap to get him to reveal himself.

"If you can hear me, Brian speak up."

Reaching down, Ten Brian picked up a small stone and tossed it in a high arc so that it would fall without revealing where it came from.

The stone fell, and Kelsey chuckled. "Now I might have knowed you'd pull somethin' like that. Anyway, it tells me what I want to know. We got to talk, Ten, just like old times."

Gun in hand, Ten Brian said, "You want to surrender, Reub? Is that it?"

"Surrender? *Me*? No, I'm offerin' you a chance to cut loose from them sodger boys and live it high out 'Frisco way. With that money we can do it."

"Reub, you know we've got you. We know you're out here now, so the army will never let up. Major Devereaux is not far away, and we can move in on you."

He chuckled again. "Can you now? I had me a run-in with your Major man a night or two ago and he come off second-best. He's got him some green hands there. My boys are all seasoned—tough lads."

He glanced over his shoulder toward the shelter. "But that gold now? Just you an' me?"

"And then just you?"

Kelsey laughed. "Damn it, no! Anybody else, maybe, but not you. After all, you an' me, were partners. We come out of the rough country together, you an' me!"

"That was a long time ago. I'll tell you what. You turn the payroll over to me and I'll see that you get a running start."

Kelsey was silent for a few minutes and then he said, "Ten, where you been all these years? I missed you around."

"Africa, China . . . a lot of places. Fighting mostly."

"No foolin'? I used to think about them places, but I never got further east than Knoxville."

He was leaning on his saddle. Brian remained hidden in the brush, but he knew that Kelsey had him located within inches. His eyes strayed toward the lean-to. Soon somebody would be coming to see what had become of Kelsey.

"Surrender now, hand over the gold, Reub, and I'll do all I can to get you a pardon. You can start fresh."

"With what? I don't need a fresh start, just a running

108

start. Can't you just see me in 'Frisco with all that money?"

Ten Brian was thinking of one thing only. He wanted to get the gold and get back to Mary, and then to the post. The rain had eased, and any minute now, some of the men would appear.

"You don't stand much of a chance of getting away with that gold," he said. "Your boys will be watching, and expecting a split."

"I'll take care of that." Kelsey paused a moment. "You got a gun on me?"

"Of course. From the beginning."

"Ain't changed much, have you? You always was a cautious one."

A man had come outside and was looking toward Kelsey. He picked up a pack saddle and went to a horse. "Stick around," Kelsey said to Brian, low-voiced. "We'll work something out."

Then he called out, "Chet? You want to lend me a hand?"

The man came over. "What's the idea? Are we gettin' out of here?"

"Just in case," Kelsey said, and as the man bent over to pick up the second pack saddle, Kelsey laid the barrel of his pistol alongside his head. The man hit the ground with a thump.

"One less," Kelsey commented. "Come and get him."

Chapter 14

Brian remained where he was. "He's yours. You take care of him."

Coolly, after a quick glance toward the lean-to, Kelsey took the man by the scruff of the neck and dragged him to the brush. Then with rawhide from his saddlebag he trussed him neatly, and gagged him. Going back, he proceeded to finish the saddling of the pack horses.

Ten Brian watched warily. Reuben Kelsey had nerve, but he would take no unnecessary risks. Brian did not trust him for one minute, knowing that he would kill him without any qualms when the need arrived. He felt that for the time being Kelsey planned to use him—how he could not guess. The two of them stood a better chance of escaping with the gold than did either one alone. Kelsey knew this.

When the saddling was completed he said, "Stick around. I'll be needin' you."

Kelsey walked back to the lean-to and when he emerged again he carried a sack of gold. Dropping it near the horses, he returned for the other sack. Heavy as they were, Brian noted that Kelsey carried them with ease, as he had handled the unconscious man earlier.

"Are they letting you get away with it?" Brian asked.

Kelsey grinned. "Playin' cards," he said, "an' they don't worry much. We been together quite a spell."

Methodically, he loaded the gold on the pack horse, then went back for the supplies.

Brian measured the distance to the horses. A quick run, a leap into the saddle, but it could not be that simple. Reuben Kelsey never took a chance on anybody. There was a catch to it somehow.

Kelsey came out of the lean-to carrying two packs, one in each hand but there was a pistol in his waistband as well as one in a holster at his belt, and undoubtedly he had others.

He grinned as he neared the horses. "Had your chance, Ten. Wonder you didn't take it."

Brian chuckled. "I figured you had an edge, although I didn't know how."

"Didn't tighten my cinch," Kelsey explained cheerfully. "If you'd jumped into the saddle you'd have fallen right off, and you'd never get that cinch tightened *and* mount up and git away before I had you in my sights."

"Anyway," Brian said, "I'm considering your idea. 'Frisco does sound appetizing."

"We'd have us a time," Kelsey agreed. "It ain't no fun, a man by hisself. You an' me, we could take that town apart. Maybe even buy ourselves a place on the Barbary Coast somewhere. That's a whole sight easier than riding day in an' day out. We could just set, sell whiskey, and let the money come rollin' in." He winked. "I hear there's money in shanghaiing sailors for them ships, too."

Where was Ironhide?

There was no sign of the Cherokee. No sound that might come from him, no evidence that he had been around the camp at all.

The horses were loaded now, the grub was packed, the gold was packed. Kelsey was just fiddling with the packs, making sure they would ride easy.

111

"You got you a horse?"

"No."

"I'll saddle the sorrel." Kelsey paused, his hand on one pack, his left hand. "You comin' with me?"

Brian eased himself to his feet, making no sound. He lifted one foot and took a step, putting it down gently. Kelsey had had him located within inches, he was sure of that, so he moved . . . ever so gently lifting the other foot.

"I said, 'Are you comin' with me?' "

Brian hesitated, uncertain as to his next move. The gold was right there in front of him, packed and ready on a horse. A saddled horse was there too.

"I take it I've wasted my breath," Kelsey said calmly. "Well, it's your grave you're diggin'."

He turned suddenly, cupping his mouth with his hands. "Duck! Reynolds! Come a-runnin'!"

Turning sharply, he let go with two fast shots at Brian's former position, ran a step and fired again as the men came boiling from the shelter.

"Up the slope. It's Brian. *Get him!*"

The men let fly with a quick volley of shots, most of which were scattered along the slope. It was the last thing Brian expected, but instinctively he did the right thing. He turned sharply and ran along the slope but not up it.

Wtih one mind the men charged into the brush, yelling. Picking up a rock, Brian hurled it far up the slope. It fell, and there was a shot, then another.

Brian looked back. Kelsey was in the saddle, holding the lead ropes on the two pack horses. He was riding away!

Stepping out of the brush, Brian lifted his rifle and took dead aim. At the same instant, Kelsey fired.

Brian felt a sharp blow on the skull; he staggered, and fell . . . he seemed to fall for a long time. When he hit the brush, he tumbled over and brought up on the

112

ground with shocking force. That was the last he remembered.

The day passed slowly in the cave. Mary Devereaux talked to Belle, helped rustle wood for the fire, and prepared food, but she could not keep herself from grim thoughts. Somewhere within a few miles of her the two men she loved most were in the gravest danger.

Schwartz was silent much of the time, but when he spoke he tried to reassure her. "The Lieutenant is a good man, a brave man. He will do nothing foolish. And wherever he is, you can be sure the Cherokee is not far away".

Nonetheless, she was worried and frightened. When night came, Schwartz stood guard most of the night, but he awakened her just before daybreak, when he could no longer keep his eyes open.

She made up her mind then. If there was not some news by noon they would move out. True, Ten had told her to wait, but her father was not far away and she might be able to get to him. Anything was better, she thought, than waiting in the cave

Schwartz did not agree. "Stay here," he warned her. "We can make no tracks here, no tracks for Kelsey's men to follow. He has many men, and they are all over the mountains, and they are evil men, like none you have ever met. We must wait."

Mary protested, but she finally gave in. They would wait one more night, and no more. Belle too was worried, but she also advised caution.

They kept the fire small, and they waited. Once, far off, they believed they heard gunfire.

Schwartz alone was calm, but he made frequent trips to the cave mouth to look about. The rain had ceased, but the clouds hung low. Water dripped from every tree. The sound of the water came up to them from the stream far below, but it was a sullen, muted sound, almost sinister, it seemed.

"Are you in love with him?" Belle asked the question suddenly.

"I . . . I think so. I don't know."

"He's quite a man."

"My father doesn't approve, but you know that. He likes him as a man and as an officer, but not as a husband for me."

They were silent for a few minutes and then Belle spoke. "Do you think they have gone back? Your father, I mean. I know they were limited as to time."

Just then Schwartz spoke. "Somebody is coming."

They drew back into the cave. Schwartz moved toward the entrance, and Mary also. They waited and listened. The horses' heads were up, ears pricked.

Schwartz lifted his rifle. Mary whispered, "Don't shoot unless you must. They may come close without finding us."

For a long time then there was no sound. Mary's lips were dry, and one leg was cramped and she desperately wanted to move it, but she was afraid to make even the slightest sound. Then she heard a low murmur of voices.

"Aw, you're havin' pipe dreams! I didn' see nothin', an' besides, there's no tracks. Nobody's come along here in years."

"Might have been a shadow, but I'd swear I saw somethin' down there just about sunup. Somethin' moved."

"Deer, maybe. There's a-plenty of them around. Have a look if you're so minded." There was a pause and the same voice continued. "Anyway, where would they be? There's no place to hide."

A moment longer they stood talking, and then there came a far-off sound of firing. It was faint, but it was unmistakable.

"Shootin'," one of the men said, "back across the hill. Now what d' you suppose that is?"

114

"We'd better go back. We got a stake in that sixty thousand, y' know."

They turned away and their footsteps receded, and then there was silence again.

"It's Ten!" Mary exclaimed. "I know it. He's in trouble!"

"There is nothing we can do," Belle said. "We must wait."

"We could help him."

"Ma'am," Schwartz said gently, "now he's got only himself to worry about, and maybe getting that payroll back. If you were over there he'd have to think about carin' for you, and that would most likely get himself killed. Believe me, ma'am, when it comes to guns a man had best have a mind for nothing but the other man and himself."

"He's right, Mary. You know he is," Belle said.

"I do know it." She turned quickly. "Schwartz, couldn't you go?"

"I could go. The trouble is by the time I got where the fightin' is it would all be over, and I would have left my post. No, ma'am. My place is here with you."

"Then let's try to get to my father."

Schwartz looked at her thoughtfully. "Miss Devereaux, I understand how you feel, but it is a wide country out there, and finding your father would not be easy. However, we can try." He paused. "But you must remember that when we leave this place nobody will know where we are."

The thought had not occurred to her, but she brushed it aside. "In the morning, then?"

"In the morning," he said, resignedly.

Daybreak was a mere lightening of the sky, for the clouds still hung low. They saddled up, and after a small breakfast, Schwartz scouted the outside again.

His comprehension of their position was vague, but he assumed it to be somewhere on the southern or western flank of the Roaring Fork Mountains. The

115

peak above them he believed to be Atlantic Peak, and thought that by striking east and keeping off the higher slopes they could reach Sioux Pass. He would, he decided, stay in the mountains, or at least in the foothills, for there was water there, and places of concealment might be found, with occasional high points to permit looking over the country.

At the moment of leaving he said, "Remember this. We must talk very little if at all. Voices carry in these canyons."

Mounting up, he led them away from the cave and along the steep path, and then he chose a dim trail that followed a bench covered with thick clumps of aspen. They crossed occasional meadows with scattered spruce. He was not very skillful at covering a trail, but he tried to leave as little sign as possible and several times went back to kick the tallest grass erect.

They were about nine thousand feet up, he thought, judging by the plant growth, and there was ample cover. By noon they had reached the headwaters of a creek that he assumed was the Little Sweetwater.

Behind a clump of aspen, sheltered from the higher slopes by scattered spruce, they dismounted. There was little breeze, and they found dry wood, so he built a small fire behind some rocks. These were frontier women with whom he rode, but they had been out now for several rough days and he had no idea how much they could take. The rest and the coffee would be good for them. While they drank coffee and rested in the sun that found a chink in the clouds, he climbed to a shoulder of the mountain.

The view to the southwest was partly obscured by a butte, but he could see glimpses that showed him the flat country sweeping away toward the Green River. Nowhere did he see any life, any movement . . . except for an eagle that soared far above on easy wings.

To the north he could see a broad blue expanse that must be a lake. The largest lake in this region of which he had heard was Christina Lake, and he felt they must be near the pass. Sioux Pass was to the south, but Brian had several times mentioned another pass that he thought was snowed in, but from this vantage point he could see only scattered patches of snow. If he took the pass above Christina Lake he could avoid well-traveled Sioux Pass and the risks of meeting Kelsey's men.

Slowly he walked back down the mountain. He could see the horses grazing on the grass below him. For some reason he thought of Germany. He paused, resting the butt of his rifle on the ground. . . . Would he ever see Germany again?

He looked down to where the horses grazed . . . but they were gone! He looked again . . . there was no sign of them, nor any sign of the women either. Quickly he caught up his rifle and took a long step off the rock on which he was standing.

It was the longest step he ever took, and the last. Something struck him a wicked blow on the spine and, his leg outstretched for the step, he seemed to go sailing, on and on as if he had taken off in flight. Distantly, the sound of a shot came to him.

He hit the grass with a jolt and rolled over. He looked up at the sky, and the sun faded. It was going to rain again, he thought, for it was suddenly growing dark. He thought of Belle Renick and Mary Devereaux then, and tried to get up, but there was no feeling in his legs.

Suddenly Mary Devereaux was bending over him. "Christina," he said distinctly, and tried to point. "Please," he said. And then, "I am sorry, ma'am." They were his last words.

Mary looked up at Belle. "He's dead," she said gently. "He was a good man, Belle."

Chapter 15

Tenadore Brian opened his eyes into a shadowed stillness, aware only of the dull throb in his skull and of the silence.

His mind was not fuzzy. Miraculously, his faculties seemed unimpaired. He was lying on a bed of leaf mold under a thick bush. Above him were broken branches, and he assumed he had fallen through the bush, which had sprung back into place, offering complete cover.

He turned his head. Less than a dozen feet away was a cluster of rocks from which water flowed. He wanted a drink badly, but he lay still, thinking about what had happened, trying to judge the time that must have elapsed. If he knew how much time had gone by he would have a better idea about his next move.

Kelsey's shot had hit him, but he did not believe he was badly hurt. His head throbbed, but whether it was from the bullet or the fall he did not know. By now Kelsey was gone and the gang might have scattered, hunting him ... or they might be around, within hearing distance. They might have searched for him, but to have found him would have meant an almost inch-by-inch search of the area, hidden as he was.

Carefully now, he turned on his side, got an elbow under himself and raised up. He crawled out from under the bush, and in so doing came upon his rifle. It had fallen into the same leaf mold and was apparently undamaged.

At the spring, he drank deep, then bathed his head. There was a scalp wound over his left ear, but the blood had congealed and there was no bleeding now. When he stood up his head swam, and for a moment he caught hold of a tree for support. When the momentary dizziness had passed, he moved through the brush and trees until he came to a spot where he was about three hundred yards from the lean-to. The horses were gone and there was nobody in sight.

Slowly, he looked around. He needed a horse, and he needed to know where his enemies were. Crouching there, he watched the lean-to for several minutes, but saw no sign of life. He stepped out of the brush then, waited a moment, and walked over to the lean-to. It was empty, and only dull coals were left of the fire.

The leave-taking had been hasty. The cards were scattered, there was a glove and a rolled up blanket someone had used for a pillow. Evidently they had rushed out, charged up the slope, and returning after a while, had found Kelsey gone, and the gold.

They would not doubt Kelsey at first—not all of them. Many of them had been with him for several years, all the way from Missouri. They would have heard the shots fired, and some of them might think he had been wounded or captured. But being the men they were, some would be suspicious that he had taken the gold and fled, and they would seek out his tracks.

Brinn roamed about the outer edges of the camp, studying the sign. Evidently some of the remaining horses had been stampeded, for he could tell that at least a dozen men had walked away from the lean-to, with frequent stops to look back.

Without horses, in Indian country, they would first attempt to secure horses, and the nearest ones were with the command of Major Devereaux. These men, experienced horse thieves, would not hesitate to make

119

an attempt to get them. Once mounted, they would probably try to come up with Kelsey.

Surely Kelsey must know this. And if he knew it, he must have planned for it.

He could, of course, lie in wait. He might kill one or more of them, but then the others would stalk him, and the odds would not be in Kelsey's favor, no matter how good a fighter he was. So he must have a hide-out somewhere ahead, or he must have friends to whom he could go, friends who would also defend him.

In this country that would mean Indians . . . unless he had planned with some of his own men, using them to cover his retreat, and then to kill the others who were following.

As to the Indians, Kelsey might have made friends among them, or even lived among them at some time, and he might return there now. The Shoshones were friendly, so it would not be that tribe he would ride toward. More likely it would be the Sioux or the Blackfeet.

It seemed to Brian that the only thing for him to do now was to go back to the cave. He had lost Kelsey, lost his own men, and he had not found Ironhide. The payroll was getting further away all the time, so he ought to go back, get his horse, then get Mary and Belle Renick back to the command. After that, no matter how cold the trail, he must hunt down Kelsey and get back the gold.

He walked slowly, for he was very tired, and his head did not cease from aching. He knew he was in serious danger, for some of the Kelsey outfit would still be in these mountains, still searching for the girls or for him. But his weariness and the throb in his head dulled his awareness, and when he stopped it was an effort to get started again.

Suddenly a pair of blue grouse burst from the brush almost at his feet, startling him so that he stumbled and almost fell. Crossing over a low shoulder, he came

120

down into a pleasant little park among the trees. A half-dozen yellow-bellied marmots were playing on the grass, but at his approach they ducked for shelter in a jumble of rocks that had tumbled from the ridge above. Stumbling, he went on across the park and paused to lean against a tree on the far side.

It would soon be night. He had to get to the cave. Once he arrived there he could sleep. He could have some hot coffee. He started on and had gone a dozen feet before he realized he had left his rifle.

Returning, he picked it up and took a slightly different direction, climbing higher toward the timberline. Twice he slipped and fell. At last he made the ragged fringe of trees where the long winds blew, and stood on the mountain top, watching the darkness close down around him.

He went through a faint golden mist of avalanche lilies, startling a white-tailed ptarmigan. Somehow he got down the slope, somehow he found the canyon, but he was only vaguely aware of what he was doing when he started down it. In his eagerness and desperation he ran a few feet, stumbling and falling against the bank. Then he went on.

Then he saw the tree. He went on, dragging the butt of his rifle. He rounded the tree. The cave was a black hole in front of him, and he went in.

It was empty. They were gone. His horse was gone, his pack was gone.

He stood still, his legs spread to preserve his balance, his eyes blinking slowly, as he tried to comprehend. Suddenly, he shivered.

The wind stirred through the canyon, moving like a presence. He dropped to his knees, fumbled some sticks together, and tried to get a fire started, but his fingers were clumsy.

At last he succeeded ... a tiny blaze. He hovered over it, coaxing it to life with crumpled leaves and bits of bark rubbed to rags between his fingers. He was

121

shaking with a chill ... was he sick? He had heard somewhere that a blow on the head sometimes disturbed a man's physical make-up and opened the way for other illnesses.

He put a little more fuel on the fire, and felt the slow warmth of it creep over him. He remembered putting his rifle down near the firewood in the corner, remembered drawing his slicker close about him, and then he remembered nothing.

He was awakened by a kick in the ribs. He started to rise, and was kicked again. He fell, tried to gather himself together, and a third kick missed his head and hit him on the shoulder, knocking him halfway around. He lay there in a nightmare of pain.

Slowly he became aware of his surroundings. Half a dozen men were in the cave ... Kelsey men. One part of his brain seemed fully conscious; the other part seemed numb, and confused by delirium.

"What kind of a setup is this?" one of the men snarled. "He ain't even got a horse! What's goin' on? You said there'd be women here!"

"They must've pulled out. I don't know who this one is."

"He's that lieutenant that Kelsey was talkin' about. The one he used to know."

"Hell, there ain't nothin' tough about *him!* Was Kelsey just leadin' us on?"

One man was crouching over the fire, building the blaze higher. Ten Brian lay on the floor of the cave, shivering, but the side of his brain that could think was seeing it all with remarkable clarity.

His rifle ... they had not seen his rifle. Nor had they searched him, and he was still wearing his pistol. The flap was buttoned down and it was underneath him. Their horses were outside.

Horses!

He lay very still, and they ignored him. He was ten feet from the rifle. It lay over there in the shadows beyond the pile of fireweed . . . if he could get to it. But he dare not move.

"You got the coffee, Jess? Let's get it started."

"Take your time." The man over the fire was cool. "We been gone from camp for quite a spell. You given that any thought?"

"What dif'rence does it make?"

"Sixty thousand in gold. That there's a lot o' money, and I been thinkin'. Supposin' you had sixty thousand dollars right by you, and you had you a horse?"

Nobody said anything, nor did they need to. Each man had his own picture, nor did any of them question what the others were thinking . . . they knew.

"What's that mean?" one of them asked.

"Well, s'posin' it happened to Kelsey, now?"

"Aw, Jess, forget it! Kelsey wouldn't leave no outfit like this! Anyway, he's got a good bit stashed back in Julesburg."

"Has he? How do you know where it is? How do we know where *he* is?"

Brian's lips shaped the words first and then he spoke. "Gone. He's taken the gold and he's heading for Salt Lake."

They turned on him. One man—the same man—booted him in the ribs again. "What d' you know about it?"

He looked up, his lips fumbling clumsily with the words. "I . . . I saw him. He . . . he shot me."

The big man drew back his foot, but Jess stopped him. "Wait!" He looked down at Brian. "He's been shot, all right, an' *we* never done it. Fact is," he said calmly, "I think he's dyin'."

They towered over him, looking at him with mild curiosity. They did not care . . . he was no danger to them. If he died, so much the better.

Jess had a look in his eyes that might have been pity. "Where was this?"

"Camp ... lean-to. He ... he shot at me. Ordered them into the brush after me."

The speech had required too much effort. Brian sank back on the floor of the cave and the others turned away from him. After a moment one of them spoke. "Makes sense," he said. "All but Salt Lake."

"He wouldn't head for Jules ... the army's that way, and there's some of our boys in Jules, too. They'd ask questions."

"Kelsey would answer them. Did you ever see him fail?"

They argued, drank coffee, and made another pot. Jess was cool, persuasive. They simply had to go back, pick up his trail, and stay with it. They'd get him.

The big man's name was Jube, and he liked none of it. He believed none of it. "He's lyin'," he said flatly.

Ten Brian eased himself over a few inches, then a few inches further. His brain was buzzing, and now he felt hot. He got his hand under his coat and laid hold of his six-shooter.

"Salt Lake," Jess said; "that don't make sense."

"It's closest. He could ride right past Bridger."

Brian made another few inches, then something in him seemed to cave in and he passed out.

When he opened his eyes his head was splitting with pain, his brain was foggy, and for a few minutes he had no idea where he was.

"Ketched 'em," a voice was saying, "Sam an' me. We seen 'em with this sodger, so we kilt him an' we taken them." And then he added, more slowly, "An' they're ours."

Comprehension fought through the fog in Brian's brain and suddenly his thoughts seemed to focus. He was down, he was in bad shape, but he had his hand on his gun and the rifle was not far away.

He turned his head. Mary and Belle stood just outside the circle of light from the fire, and he could see a man's boots, the man who guarded them—probably Sam.

These were the men who had wiped out the wagon train, who had raped, murdered, and mutilated women and children. No worse lot of renegades lived ... and they had Mary.

Chapter 16

"That's right," Jube said. "They're ours."

Ten Brian moved again and scored a couple of inches. He tried again, and moved a little more. He was closer, but the chips were down and unless he was mistaken all hell was going to break loose within minutes.

"Don't you pull that, Jube!" Sam's voice cracked like a whip.

"The young one is her that Kelsey was huntin'. You boys ready to cross him?"

There was a moment of stillness while this soaked in. Sam said, "We ketched them—not him."

"You tell that to him," Jess said. "He'll be around."

Nobody had anything to say to that, and Brian inched a little closer to the rifle. The man nearest to him, with his back squarely to him, wore two pistols. Those pistols were better at this range than the rifle, so if shooting started he had to have those guns.

"Bring 'em in," Jube said. "Let's see what you caught."

The girls were here. Kelsey was far away, and perhaps they would not see him again. Not even Jess would persuade these men to wait. There had been too much of that, and this was an undisciplined lot.

There would be no mercy for Belle or Mary, and

none for himself. He knew what had been done to the women and children of the wagon trains. These men were more savage than any savage. Kelsey had deliberately chosen men who had no qualms, such men as only he could control.

Easing himself a little, Brian got the pistol further forward, just under the cover of his slicker. There he lay, waiting.

"Bring 'em in!" Jube yelled.

"Like hell!"

Suddenly the women vanished, jerked back out of the light by Sam. "Like hell," he said. "We got to have an understandin'."

"Sure, Sam," Jube said slyly, "we understand you. We understand everythin' you say. You just come in here an' put down your gun an' we'll talk this thing out, man to man."

Sam stepped back into the cave entrance. The other man, whoever he was, remained outside, guarding the women.

"We ketched those women," Sam repeated, "an' they're ours, to keep or trade as we want."

"We can talk this out, Sam. You just put down your gun an' set down."

Sam hesitated, then shrugged. These were men he had fought beside, men he had gambled with and looted with, men he knew. He lowered his rifle and half-turned to lean it against the cave wall. When his eyes shifted back, Jube held a gun. He was smiling.

"You're too trustin', Sam. Don't ever let nobody talk you into puttin' down your gun least he does likewise. Now, what was we sayin'?"

Jess and the other men had moved back a little. Each watched Jube and Sam.

"Now, Sam," Jube said, "you call the breed. Tell him to bring those women in here . . . now."

"Wait a minute, Jube! We was goin' to talk this over!"

"That was when you held a gun," Jube replied. "You got no bargainin' position now, boy. You done give it up. I can shoot you before you can get that belt gun out . . . you always did wear it wrong. I can shoot you dead. You call that breed."

"I ain't a-goin' to do it," Sam said. "We made a deal."

Jube chuckled. "Sam, you're a fool. You can't deal with a man that holds all the cards. All you can do is take what he offers . . . if you're lucky enough to get offered anythin'. You call that breed."

"He won't come. I told him not to come in or let those girls come unless I came out after him . . . alone."

Jube smiled. "You just turned over your last card, boy," he said, "an' she's nothin' but a deuce. You get up on your feet an' you walk right outside the cave. The minute you're out, you tell him to come on in."

"And then what?"

"Like I say, you got no bargainin' position. I hold the gun."

Sam got up slowly and walked to the mouth of the cave. Hesitating, he glanced back. The black muzzle of the gun was on him like a single ugly eye. He stepped outside. "Jason," he called, "bring 'em in!"

He spoke, then leaped. He sprang for the darkness and the edge of the cliff, over which there was a short slide to a narrow ledge, then a drop-off of fifty feet or more. He knew this and took his chance, for once over the rim he would be out of danger.

His feet hit the edge instead of going over, and Jube's bullet caught him at the same time. He landed on his feet, lifted on his toes, and fell outward, his head tilting down, and then he was gone.

With a rush, the men in the cave burst from its mouth, and Ten Brian, scrambling to his feet and catching up his rifle, followed.

He knew about the ledge, and he knew it was his one

chance, unsteady though he was. He went forward and went over the edge as the renegades scattered in search of the girls. Clinging to the rounded face, he let himself slide over, his feet feeling for the ledge below. Finding it, he worked himself along the face of the cliff. He could hear the searchers thrashing in the brush. He reached a wider corner of the ledge and paused to rest. He was dizzy, and his head felt like a drum. He had clung to his rifle, and holstered the pistol.

Sam had called the half-breed Jason . . . Brian knew him. Jason had spent much time around the Fort, and was often in Julesburg. Several times Brian had bought him drinks. When around the Fort he had undoubtedly been spying for Kelsey, but that was unimportant now. Jason had also served as a scout for the army on numerous occasions, and once had been a scout on a long march into the country north of Laramie led by Brian himself.

Ten Brian clung to the face of the cliff, waiting until his dizziness passed. He wanted nothing so much as to lie down and rest.

But there could be no rest. Jason had the girls with him and he might try to escape or might not, but with so many men hunting for him, they were almost sure to come upon them.

After a few minutes he climbed off the ledge by a watercourse, scrambling up over the small boulders, trying to make no noise. Twice he was forced to stop and wait until his head stopped spinning.

Jason would, he decided, go up the mountain rather than down into a canyon which might be impassable, or along the trail where he was sure to be caught. The mountainside was covered with patches of aspen, with small open areas here and there and some spruce. Crossing the trail, Brian went up the steep slope through the trees.

His wound was slight—of that he was sure—but the blow on his head had been a severe shock, and he was

129

suffering from exposure and lack of food. He paused once to listen, then climbed on through the trees.

He crouched at the base of a spruce, hidden by its low-hanging branches, and tried to catch his breath. The sky was overcast and no stars were visible. Somewhere on the slope above him would be Jason with Belle and Mary. What would the half-breed do?

That he might be an outlaw Brian was prepared to accept, but he had always considered Jason a man to be respected, and he had an idea that Jason had deliberately chosen his moment to help the girls escape, though on that he might be mistaken.

He wanted to give himself the advantage of distance, and after a few minutes he went on up the slope. He doubted if they would waste much time searching for him—it was Belle and Mary whom they wanted to find, but if they came upon him they would kill him . . . if they could.

Finally, he could go no further. Under the ground-touching limbs of a spruce, he made a bed of spruce needles and grass, then crawled close to the tree trunk, and with his rifle held close, he went to sleep.

Cold awakened him, but there was a grayness in the sky that warned dawn was near, and already he could make out the outlines of trees and rocks. He wiped his guns free of moisture. He had no illusions about his chances, which grew less by the hour. His own condition was not good, he was without a horse in a country where a horse was the first essential, and he was surrounded by enemies. If by some chance he escaped them, there were still the Indians. During the past few months there had been continual fights with the Sioux, Cheyennes, and Arapahoes all along the trail from mid-Kansas to Fort Bridger.

He peered from beneath the tree for a long time before he crawled out, but when he tried to straighten up he was so stiff that it took him some time to stand up. Yet, surprisingly, he felt better. His head still ached, but not so much, and the sleep had done him good.

He studied the ground for tracks, cutting across the flank of the mountain to intercept the trail of anybody attempting to climb over. He found the tracks of a dozen men, but none at all that seemed to be those of women.

He thought of Jason, who he knew was shrewd. He would think of pursuit, would find some way to evade it.

The bare bones of the mountain above timberline rose only a few hundred yards away, and before him was a long talus slope. He crossed this and moved into the low-growing spruce beyond. From that point he could see over into the canyon. Far below, he saw a dozen elk moving across an open meadow and into the trees. But something nearer by drew his attention. A spike of red elephant, already budded although it was early in the season, had been pushed down and crushed. The flower stem had almost straightened up, but the mark of a heel was still upon it.

Without moving, he searched the ground carefully a few steps beyond, and after a moment found the merest suggestion of a track in loose gravel. He started on, pausing at every other step to let his eyes examine the terrain. Indications were scanty, but they were there, though of one person only.

He cut for sign, moving right and left, circling warily. After several minutes he found it . . . another track.

He could guess what had happened. The two women and Jason were walking widely separated so as to leave no definite trail. He needed to follow only one of them, so he kept on, working forward quickly, despite frequent pauses to see just what he might be walking into.

The trail led across the slope at the foot of the talus; the tracks had been made only hours before. He followed them over the ridge, then paused to scan the country before him. Far off was the blue of Lake

131

Christina, in front of him a jumble of peaks. Beyond that he could get a glimpse of the open country of Deer Park.

Squatting on his heels he studied the country for a trail. There were patches of trees, open meadows along the mountainside, and then thick forest. Through the grass of the slope he could see the marks where people had passed. The tracks led into the trees close by. The head of the Little Sweetwater was on his left and behind him; Sioux Pass was to the right.

Suddenly, four men came out of the brush below him, cutting across the slope from the direction of Sioux Pass. They were well spread out, and were obviously trying to pick up a trail.

As they drew nearer, one of them yelled and pointed. There was a puff of smoke, a sharp report, and the riders scattered, dropping from their saddles as they went. Another shot followed close on the first.

Ten Brian came up off the ground with a rush and made the first clump of trees. He went through them swiftly, spotting the nearest man, who was below him, and continued down the slope, running lightly.

When he was no more than a hundred yards away, the man heard him and turned sharply. Brian had come to a halt, and as the man turned his rifle was lifting. Brian caught his front sight on the glint of a coat button, and felt the rifle jump in his hands. The man backed up and fell, hitting the ground hard.

Brian dropped to the ground, crawled swiftly ahead and to the left, then turned slightly toward where the next man had dropped. A moment before he had glimpsed him from the corner of his eye, but now the man was gone.

Brian moved again. In the excitement of action his aches and pains were gone. He thought he heard movement near by . . . he stopped and the noise stopped. He started to move again, stopped quickly, and the noise stopped, but just too slow, in the brush below him.

Instantly he lifted his rifle and put three well-directed shots where the sound had been, one in the middle, the others right and left.

No sound, no shot in return. He worked his way down the slope. Cutting through a patch of ragwort and monkey flowers, he rounded a patch of spruce and looked where his bullets had gone. A man was sitting there with a pistol in his hand, and they saw each other at the same instant.

Both fired.

Brian felt the angry whip of a bullet, and his own bullet, fired from waist-high, smashed the man back to the ground. There was blood on his thigh already. He moved in, his rifle ready for another shot. He caught a movement on his right and whirled, dropping to a crouch, but a bullet struck the man and he turned, dropping his rifle to take two slow steps before he fell.

The fortunate shot had come from down slope.

Ten Brian was down near the man he had killed, wrenching loose his gunbelt. Taking the man's pistol, he thrust it into his waistband, then putting his own rifle down he lifted the dead man's rifle and emptied it where he had last seen the other men. Dropping the empty gun, he took up his own and moved again, in a long-striding run down the slope through the trees.

Nearing where he thought they might be he paused to listen, then called softly, immediately rolling over on the ground.

A voice came back. It was Mary. Rifle ready for anything he moved down to them. Jason was there, a bloody rag around his left arm, his gaunt face hard-drawn but welcoming.

"I try to get them away, Lieutenant," the half-breed said.

"I knew you would, Jason. When I heard you were with them I worried no more."

"I have been a bad man, I think," Jason said. "I have helped Reuben Kelsey."

133

"What you have done now," Brian replied, "has made my memory bad. Your heart is good, Jason. I have always known that."

The wounded man got up, and took his rifle. "We go then?"

"We go."

Brian looked from Mary to Belle. "You've had a rough time, but we're on our way back now."

They went down the slope to the horses. Jason had them all—his own, Brian's gray, and the others. They mounted up and, hidden among the trees, moved on down the slope. There was a trail below that would help.

Now he must get the girls back to Major Devereaux. Then it would be time enough to go after the gold.

As he rode, he reloaded his guns.

Chapter 17

Between South Pass and Fort Laramie half a dozen telegraph stations had been set up, each guarded, as a rule, by four soldiers. One of the missions of the troops stationed at Fort Laramie was to protect that line as well as the stages that traveled the route.

It had taken the Indians no time at all to discover the importance of the telegraph line, and they were constantly tearing it down, burning the poles, and carrying off the wire to be made into bracelets or other ornaments.

Buffalo were also a threat to the line, for they found the slender poles all too convenient for scratching purposes, and frequently they pushed over the poles while scratching. Needless to say, the telegraph line was an uncertain medium of communication.

The situation had become so serious that both the telegraph line and the stage line were being shifted south, away from the mountains that sheltered the raiding Indians.

Major Devereaux had gone into camp at the edge of the small community of South Pass. It was headquarters for miners working nearby creeks, and for a few hunters, and it was a stopping place for westbound wagons. When Major Devereaux had started west one of his duties was to repair the line, and to relieve the various guards, leaving men of his own in their places.

The line was in working order when he arrived at South Pass, and he sent a report to Lt. Col. Collins. He was instructed to purchase provisions at South Pass, if available, to continue his search for three days, and then to return to the Fort, following the line of the telegraph.

He was further instructed to place Lieutenant Tenadore Brian under arrest and return him to Fort Laramie for an inquiry, perhaps for a court-martial.

There had been, he was informed, Indian raids all along the line and several hundred horses had been stolen from the stage company. An emigrant train had been wiped out.

Lieutenant Cahill returned, but he had little to report. He had located a camp where the Kelsey men had evidently stopped for several days, and had found a man bound and gagged in the brush, a man who had no very coherent story of how he had come there.

There had been a brief, indecisive engagement with a party of Kelsey men in which two of the enemy were killed and one of his own men wounded. There they had been joined by Ironhide, wounded and emaciated. Ironhide had made an effort to recover the payroll, had tried to intercept Kelsey, who was escaping with it, but he had been ambushed, getting a bullet in his leg. Crawling into the brush, Ironhide had waited until Kelsey was gone, them improvised a crutch and started back. He had seen nothing of either Lieutenant Brian or the women. He had heard shooting on several occasions when working his way back across the mountains.

Major Devereaux was in a quandary. He had taken up a position for his command headquarters in the hotel at South Pass, a small frame building of half a dozen rooms. He used the main-floor room which did duty as a lobby and hotel office. He was puzzled as to his next move, for any move might well be a wrong

136

one. Though it seemed that the Kelsey force was breaking up, he had little evidence except the brief skirmish Cahill had had with an apparently leaderless group of them, and reports that several others had been seen, scattered and apparently without a uniform direction.

If Mary and Belle were with Brian they were in good hands . . . but were they? And where were they? Combing the mountains for them was out of the question. He must keep his command intact, both for its own safety and for any military move they might have to make.

Brian might bring the girls here, though he might try for Fort Bridger, or even try to return to Fort Laramie. But he would have no reason to feel there would be no safety in South Pass. The population of the town was small, constantly in fear of Indian attack, and unable to withstand an attack by Kelsey's band if it could still muster its former number.

Undoubtedly Kelsey had spies in the town. In fact the very hotel which Major Devereaux was using as temporary headquarters was questionable. There had been rumors about it, and the Major had no liking for the woman who operated the place.

The door opened and Turpenning stepped in. "Suh?"

"What is it, Turpenning?"

"Request puhmission, suh, to go a-scoutin'. Figure I might find the Lieutenant, suh, an' maybe Miss Mary and the Captain's wife."

"Permission refused, Turpenning, but I appreciate the offer, and the risk it would entail." He placed his pen on the table. "We have other fish to fry, Turpenning. There is some likelihood that the Kelsey gang may have broken up or scattered, and we are going to round up as many of them as possible. It is important their sort of action be ended, once and for all."

"Yes, suh."

"I am sending Cahill out with ten men, and Corpor-

137

al Chancel with another ten. You will accompany Lieutenant Cahill."

When Turpenning had left, Devereaux sat back and stared out at the bleak hills where the green was just beginning to show. Even now Mary might be fighting for her life somewhere in the mountains. . . .

Within a fifty-mile radius there must be fifty or a hundred canyons, scores of remote parks, and many streams, and most of it covered with forest. Where to look among all that? A thousand men might do it, in several weeks. He dare not risk the small parties at his command in such a venture, no matter how willing they were to go.

He must trust to Lieutenant Tenadore Brian, the man he disliked. At this moment there was no one else.

He felt old and tired. He looked at the reports he had been writing, but his eyes would not focus, nor his mind. He could only think of Mary, somewhere out there.

Mary . . . he remembered her as a tiny girl, as she had been when Madge was alive. He had no right to expose Mary to this, and once she was back—if she ever came back—he must take her back east where she could have the sort of life a woman needs. The frontier was too harsh. It was no life for a young girl.

If he only had another chance!

He could retire. He need not finish his years out as a soldier. There were other things he could do. Only a few years ago his brother had offered him a job . . . he needed someone to manage a construction project. He would, he must get away from this.

Beyond the bleak hills were the mountains, not far off, waiting for him. He had always loved the mountains, loved them as Madge had loved them, and as Mary, too, did love them. That was the trouble, of course, with thinking of leaving. There was always the vast distance with the grass bending in the wind, the whispering leaves of the aspens, the gold of them when

138

autumn came. How could a man who had known such vast distance confine himself to a desk? To the crowded streets of an eastern town?

He remembered the first time he had seen the Plains. For days they rode westward, day after day the open land, always stretching before them. They had called it the Great American Desert, but it was no desert . . . there was grass everywhere. And the buffalo . . . thousands of wild horses running free . . . antelope. And along the rivers the giant cottonwoods.

He got up, feeling strangely alone, and walked outside.

The air was cool and fresh off the mountains, with a smell of pines. Across the dusty street a horse stamped and flagged his tail against the flies. A man in miner's boots came out of the store and stood on the steps, and two men in uniform rode in from camp.

It was his life, and he would not want to leave it. He stood for a moment, fumbling with a cigar. Finally he lighted it and then went back inside and seated himself at the desk again. He thought of Kelsey . . . Reuben Kelsey. The man must be found, for such a man was too dangerous to be allowed to run free.

Before the day was over one of his patrols returned with two prisoners, and a report of a fight where two men had been killed. The prisoners could tell him nothing . . . or they would not. But after questioning he was doubtful that they had anything to tell. They said they had been scouting, trying to locate Lieutenant Brian and the payroll. Then word came to them that the payroll had been taken and they started for the rendezvous near the Little Sweetwater, only to find it abandoned.

Of one thing he was now sure. The Kelsey gang, for whatever reason, had come apart at the seams. The men were scattering, trying to lose themselves. Or perhaps they were scouting for Kelsey himself.

"Sir," Cahill suggested, "I think Kelsey took the money and left—on his own."

"I am inclined to agree." Devereaux's brow furrowed, and Cahill, who loved him like a father, winced at the older man's face. It had thinned down and he looked years older. "When the other patrol comes in, have Corporal Chancel report to me."

A trapper, who had worked the northern stretches of the Wind River range came in to South Pass City. Anybody who went north was a fool, he said. The Sioux and the Blackfeet were ranging all that country, and coming south he had only barely avoided more than one war party.

"I ain't a-goin' to trap no more," he told Cahill over a buffalo meat stew in the restaurant. "Beaver's trapped down to where they got barely enough left to reproduce theirselves."

He chewed thoughtfully. "I seen nobody up yonder but Injuns, but anybody who is in that country better get out, an' fast. I never seen so many redskins in all my born days."

He paused and looked up. "Come to think of it, I did see somethin' almighty curious up there. A few years back I found a cave up there and somebody had done a sight of work around, walling it up. He had him a cache in there, too—ammunition, tools, and grub . . . tinned goods, and such. Looked like somebody aimed to hole up there.

"Well, a-comin' down across that country due east of the Lizard Head, I come on some tracks. Two, three hosses . . . only one of them shod. Those were fresh tracks I seen."

"Some other trapper, perhaps?"

"Ain't nobody trappin' that country no more. Nobody 'cept me, and that there's high, lonesome country. No reason for anybody goin' in there, even."

"Is there a trail across the divide?"

"Sure is. I favor the Big Sandy Trail . . . some trap-

140

per called it Jackass Trail because anybody but a jack-ass would be a fool to try it. It ain't that bad—a man afoot or on a good mountain hoss ain't liable to have trouble."

Cahill reported to Major Devereaux. "Sir, it may be just a hunch, but who would be likely to be up that way but Kelsey? He seems to have dropped from sight, and my guess is that he has the payroll, has abandoned his men, and has headed north. He may try to hide out up there until the search for him is over, and until his men have scattered and the Indians have gone away."

It made sense. Devereaux hesitated to risk the men required, with the country about to be overrun by hostiles, but he might recover the payroll, and one more foray into the mountains might locate Mary. He held back. . . . Was he trying to find reason to send them out simply because he wanted an excuse for another hunt for her?

Major Devereaux studied the map, and sent for the trapper.

A lean, raw-boned man in fringed buckskins. A man with a hard jaw and narrow eyes, uneasy inside a room, at home only in the wilderness.

"That Jackass Trail now . . . can you tell us how to locate it from the west?"

"Ain't no trouble. It's rough . . . you better take some horses you can trust on a mean trail. One place you better look at. Might want to camp there yourself, but if this gent should take a notion to leave, he might just hide out there a spell."

He put the stub of a finger on the map—the end of the finger lost by knife or trap. "After the trail crosses this here creek—North Creek, we call it—about a hundred an' fifty feet up the creek, an' west you'll find you as neat a hide-out as a man could wish. Granite all around . . . you could camp fifty men in there, if need be, an' nobody the wiser.

"But you better watch for Injuns. They scout around

141

up there, for on a clear day a body can see wagons on the Oregon Trail from up above there, on the peaks."

Major Devereaux pushed back his chair and spoke to Cahill. "Is there any word from Corporal Chancel?"

"Not yet, sir."

"Very well. Lieutenant, I shall want twenty men who are in good shape, twenty picked horses, and I shall want pack horses to carry a hundred rounds per man and rations for five days."

"You, sir?"

"Yes, Lieutenant Cahill. I shall take the patrol myself. You will remain in command here. Keep a close lookout. No man is to go more than half a mile from the town, and only upon your orders."

"But, sir, I would—"

"Lieutenant Cahill, you have your orders. That will be all."

He turned to the trapper. "How would you like to guide us? Scout's pay and a bonus?"

The mountain man shook his head. "No, *suh!* I come out of that country with my hair. I don't figure to risk it against what I seen up thataway. No, *suh.* Not for no money."

Major Devereaux shuffled his papers together, looking once more at the map. They would camp the first night out at Blucher Creek; the second in that granite basin or the vicinity. The third day they would be at the cave the trapper had mentioned, and two days back . . . if all went well.

Chapter 18

From a clump of pines on the slope of the mountain, Tenadore Brian squatted on his heels and studied the terrain below with his glasses.

There had been some good rains, and the grass was green. The young bucks would soon be riding south for the taking of scalps.

During the past few days Brian and the girls, as well as West, Dorsey, and the others, had left their tracks down there in the basin of the Little Popo Agie and around Deer Park. No Indian would miss those tracks, and even a young Indian boy could tell when they were made.

So the Indians would be down there, and might already be hunting them. The Kelsey men would be there, too, not wanting to lose a prey so close at hand. Form now on every move must be made with the greatest care, every bit of shelter utilized.

Jason moved up beside him. His face looked gray and drawn; obviously he was suffering pain from his wounded arm. "It is not good," he said. "Many hostiles, I think."

Brian handed him the glasses. "Along the shoulder of the mountain"—he pointed—"I think there is a way."

"Trails were made where men could walk," Jason

said, "I think all the places for trails have been found, and it is best to keep to a trail."

"Look carefully," Brian said. "There may have been a trail there, long ago."

Jason looked. "Maybe," he said doubtfully. "It is a chance, and we must take a chance. If you say we go ... we go."

Ten Brian led the way, walking the gray down toward the grassy ledge they had seen from above, which had seemed to lead around the mountain overlooking the lake below. The way might be treacherous, but if it was possible to follow it, it would take them above any Indians and would advance them several miles before they must descend to lower, more dangerous levels. At the same time he knew how risky what he attempted was ... they might come to the end of the ledge and find no way to go ahead, or the way might have been cut off by a slide.

Through a thick grove of aspen, they went on down emerging at last on an open slope.

They had been going only a few minutes when Jason said, "There was a trail long ago, I think."

There was a thread of bare soil here and there, a way between the rocks, a gap among the trees.

For perhaps a mile the way opened gradually before them, and they rode easy in their saddles. Then Brian drew up, looking with calculating eyes at the wide slide of shale that lay before them. It was at least a hundred yards across, with snow here and there. On the far side there seemed to be the ghost of a trail.

"I will go first," Brian said. "We will use our ropes, I think."

"There isn't enough rope, is there?" Belle asked.

"No," he replied, "but it may help to use what we have. Mary, will you follow me?"

"Yes," she said quietly.

He took a turn around his saddle horn with the rope.

"Do the same," he said, "and hold the free end. If you have to cut loose, do it."

He moved the gray toward the slide. The horse snorted and turned away, but he swung it back. Gingerly, the gray stepped out. The shale slid, but the horse only snorted and waited a moment, then started on, its hoofs seeming to find a grip on something beneath the shale.

They moved ahead slowly, and Brian could feel the tenseness of the horse under him. The shale slid a little more and they could hear the sound of it falling far below.

The gray horse went forward, more quickly now. Brian felt a slight tug on the rope and he glanced back. Mary was starting. Her horse was smaller, and very easy on its feet. He looked ahead, and had a moment of panic. The big gray was hesitating, for directly ahead the slide dipped down much more steeply, in a shallow place that had not been visible from their starting point. No more than twenty feet across, it cut at least two or three feet deeper into the mountain than the rest of the slide.

"All right, boy," Brian said. "Two jumps now. Take it quick and easy."

Whether the gray knew what he was saying or not, it seemed to sense there was no turning back. Once a wild mustang, there were few things the horse might not have attempted in its lifetime. Now it stepped forward, picking its feet high.

The shale slid in a swift cascade. The gray leaped forward, seemed scarcely to touch the surface before it sprang again, then scrambled up the other side. The big horse stood still, trembling. Behind it the shale roared by in a rush.

Brian turned in his saddle. "Mary, if your horse starts to go, grab the rope and hang on. I can pull you in."

The mare hesitated, wanting to be with the big gray,

but fearing the slide. Then suddenly, almost too suddenly, it stepped forward, and quickly, almost gaily, the small horse went across and scrambled up.

Brian gathered in the rope. "Go ahead," he said. "You can make it alone from here. I've got to stay and help the others."

She rode on without a question. There was still some fifty yards of the shale for her to cross, but this was less steep, and he watched her climb her horse up the bank and wait.

He looked back to where Belle was waiting. She was riding a tough buckskin, a mountain horse if there ever was one, which had belonged to one of the Kelsey men.

"Come on," he said, and watched her start, moored by the rope on Jason's saddle.

He suddenly realized that Jason had only one good hand, but Belle's buckskin had seen the other horses cross and showed no inclination to be left behind. It came on at once, though warily, walking with careful steps as if it knew shale slides, as no doubt it did.

At the hollow it halted, not liking the look of it. Brian made a loop and tossed it. Belle caught it deftly and took a turn around the saddle horn. Jason was coming up behind her, and she cast off his rope. The buckskin hesitated, then came on, scrambling across the hollow, but sending a roaring slide of shale down the mountain.

Brian gathered in his rope and looked across at the half-breed. For a moment their eyes held. Jason's horse was as heavy as the gray—a good, solid horse, but not as agile as the others.

Brian flipped a loop and Jason caught it. "Take a turn," Brian advised, and when the Indian had done so he added, "Tie a loop around your chest with your rope after you flip me the end."

Jason did as he was told. He flipped the loop across, then tied a loop around his body under his arms.

146

"They are behind us," he said. "I have heard them coming."

"I know it," Brian agreed, "so you'd better start."

He took a quick turn around the horn with the first rope, made the second fast to his own body.

Jason's big horse snorted, and backed away, almost into the slide behind him. He touched him lightly with the spurs and the horse leaped awkwardly ahead, hit the slide, and began to go.

The gray, a good roping horse, felt the tension coming and braced itself. The other horse hit the end of the rope, scrambled madly, then fell. Above it the slide gave way and tons of shale come roaring down. Jason sprang free of the horse and Brian grabbed the taut rope to help the gray, straining every muscle.

The shale roared by and left Jason hanging by the rope. Slowly, Brian started his horse forward, pulling the half-breed up the slope.

Suddenly Jason's feet gave way and he fell. The rope fouled his wounded arm and he screamed.

"Steady, boy!" Ten Brian slipped from the saddle.

Jason hung limp at the rope's end, lying against the face of the slide; he seemed to have fainted.

Brian turned and looked at the gray's position. There was no way the horse could move any further without being out on the slide beyond this little corner of solid earth they stood upon. The slide beyond offered only footing for a precarious crossing, not for a hard pull.

He eased forward, trying to find a place to brace himself, but each time he tried to dig in his heels the shale gave way under him.

He looked at the wounded man, who was regaining consciousness. Turning his head, Jason looked up. His teeth were bared in pain, his features twisted by it.

"Cut me loose," he said hoarsely. "Don't try it."

"Don't be a damn fool!" Brian said. "I'm going to get you up here and I'll need your help."

"Can't do it," the Indian whispered thickly.

147

"Damn you, Jason!" Brian exploded. "You do what you're told."

The half-breed looked up at him and suddenly he grinned. "All right. I'll try."

Brian glanced across the slide. What Jason had said was true. Several riders sat their horses there, watching.

There was no way to get the wounded man up without considerable banging about. The gray stood on what seemed to be the only solid ground on the whole slide, and there was room for little more than the horse. Taking a turn around his forearm with the rope, Brian braced himself, feeling with one foot for a spot that would offer him some leverage, and he found a knob of rock projecting from under the shale.

Did he dare trust it? ... he passed the rope around his shoulders, then testing his foot against the rock, he began to pull.

He knew the outlaws were watching, but he could not afford to give them any attention. Hand over hand, using all his strength, he eased the wounded man up the face of the shale. Jason managed to help with his feet from time to time, and slowly, slowly, Brian was bringing him up.

Suddenly Mary called, softly. "Ten! Be careful!"

He glanced quickly around, and saw that one of the outlaws had lifted his rifle. But he was not aiming at them, but at something above them. Looking over his shoulder he gasped and a wave of panic swept over him.

At the head of the shallow draw that had given them so much trouble there was now a steep bank of shale seven or eight feet high, which must weigh tons. As he stared, the outlaw fired. The bullet struck, but nothing happened.

Turning back to the half-breed, Brian eased the rope on his shoulders, and started again, hand over hand. He must get Jason up to relative safety before that mass of shale gave way.

148

There came another shot and he felt the rush of air preceding the slide. He braced himself, and with all his power pulled the wounded man up.

With a *whoof* of wind, the shale rushed by, taking a sweep at Jason's feet, and then Brian had him up and almost in his lap. Shakily, Brian got up, and helped Jason to stand.

Brian nodded to the gray. "Get up, Jason. He'll take you across."

"What of you?"

"I'll trust my feet. Get going now, before they start shooting at us."

Jason gave him a look. "Thanks," he said.

"Get going, damn you!" Brian said roughly. "And let them have a look at that arm when you get over there."

Brian watched the gray carry him safely across, then turned his eyes down the slope at something the others had not seen.

The slide that surrounded him widened as it descended, and seventy or eighty yards below, on the very lip of the precipice a small ledge jutted out. On it was a single tree, and beside the tree stood the horse Jason had been riding. Below the horse shale had spilled over into the void. Behind it was a stretch of shifting, uneasy shale.

The big horse was trapped. Without help it would die there.

Brian knew his own gray would have tried the shale, but the gray had been a mustang, accustomed to finding its own way out of difficulties. Jason's was a cavalry horse, and had no such background.

Tenadore Brian was no man to see an animal die if it could be helped. But what could he do? How could he even get to where it was? He might slide down the shale, but suppose he slid so fast that he was swept past the spot where the horse stood?

He looked around for something to use, and saw,

149

somewhat above him on the shale, a branch about nine feet long and as thick as his wrist. At the edge of the shale he poked and pushed gently, with infinite care, until he got it to move. As the shale moved the branch came closer, and at last he got his hands on it.

Then he stepped out on the shale, and with the pole as a brake and as something to steer with, he guided himself down to the ledge.

Once there, he put down the pole and began to talk to the horse to calm its fear, caressing it gently.

Safety lay in a dozen feet of margin between where he must cross and the cliff edge. Safety was a spot of solid earth and grass with some brush and trees, a spot that widened back into the slope of the mountain.

There was no use wasting time. The only way to get the horse across was to ride it over. He put a foot into the stirrup and swung into the saddle. He looked to his right, and there lay a vast, empty distance, a blue distance showing trees far below. He could see where they must hit first if they fell, a sandy slide hundreds of feet down.

He gathered the reins. "All right, boy," he said confidently, "we're going to do it now. We'll start up slope a little. Come on, let's go."

The horse blew through its nostrils, and took a tentative step. He nudged it with his heel, and the big horse struck out boldly.

Instantly the shale began to slide, but the horse was committed, and it buck-jumped forward, plunging up hill. Carried down, it still kept plunging up, and suddenly they were across and the horse was scrambling up on the finger of earth, there to stand trembling and frightened.

Behind them shale rattled and fell. Far below, they could hear it hitting.

Tenadore Brian mopped the sweat from his face and said, "All right, boy, let's go join the others."

Chapter 19

Reuben Kelsey sat hunched upon a flat rock well hidden among the stunted spruce of the high mountains. He held powerful field glasses, and he was studying the country about him with care.

He was well pleased with himself. The hide-out on the mountainside just below him was well hidden, and well provisioned, a result of years of careful planning.

He had begun the planning even before coming out from Missouri. The war would be over, and he was wise enough to know the Confederacy could not win. They had the best riders, the best shots, and the most willing fighting men, but they did not have the factories, the mines, or the staying power the North had.

Reuben Kelsey had only one loyalty, and that was to himself. The soldiers, North and South, would be turned loose on the country to fend for themselves. He had no intention of being one of them. From the first, while giving the impression of a free spender, he began hoarding a little. And at first it had been very little, for the pickings in the border states were small indeed. The west-bound caravans promised better, and from the first they had done well.

He had managed to get a little of his money into banks, but most of it he changed into gold—in short supply in the Mid-West—and when he moved west with his renegades, he carried it with him.

Drawn to the country where he had been as a boy, he had made many scouting trips into the mountains and had finally located the half-walled cave on War Bonnet. He had spent several days there, building up the wall, and making a cabin that was wind-tight.

Later he returned, bringing the first of the tools and supplies. He worked on the cabin, building it better, hiding it more effectively. Several times he had come, always bringing more supplies, and always approaching from a different direction so as to establish no pattern. He saw no tracks except rarely those of unshod ponies.

Now he was here, holed up to wait until the search for him had let up, and the war parties of spring had dwindled. Then he would come down out of the hills and ride the Oregon Trail, joining some wagon train until he reached the coast. From Astoria or Portland he would take a steamboat for San Francisco.

He had erased his tracks as effectively as possible, and subsequent showers had helped. He was hidden securely, and there was no need to shoot game. He was not worried about his former followers. Without his strong hand they would break up and scatter. Anyway, he had done nothing but what any one of them would have done, given the chance.

Hardly any of his former men would be dangerous. Jess ... yes, and perhaps one or two others. Nor was the army a source of worry. They would have to be patrolling back toward the east, and before they could divert anyone to hunt for him he would be long gone out of the country. The Indians were his chief worry. He had cultivated some friends among them, but he trusted them not at all.

He had only to sit tight, move around as little as possible, and wait. He lit his fire only at night when the thin trail of smoke could not be seen, and it was hidden

152

within the rock walls. He had, he decided, thought of everything.

With the money he had brought along he had something over seventy thousand dollars in gold, and half a dozen rings and watches of varying degrees of value.

He eased back now on the flat rock, reached in his pocket for a plug of tobacco, and bit off a chew. In the past he had chewed tobacco rarely, but now he did not want to smoke. He chewed and spat, and took up his glasses.

Suddenly his breath caught.

Indians. A war party of at least twenty of them was bunched near the river. They were three miles or more from his hide-out, only visible as a small patch of color. He watched them for several minutes, and then saw them ride away toward the south.

Even at that distance, they worried him. What he dreaded most of all was such a party coming up the narrow valley heading for one of the passes.

He slid down from the rock and made his way to the hide-out.

In the black of the night, he awoke sweating. For a long time he lay still, listening. He could hear the wind coming down the pass, and once he heard a rumble far off up the mountain. Thawing had loosened a rock and the wind set it rolling.

After a while he got out of bed and peered out of the loopholes. . . . Nothing. . . .

But what had awakened him? He wanted a light, but dared not strike one. If there was an Indian prowling about he might smell the smoke.

He waited for several minutes, and then returned to the warmth of his bed. For some time he lay awake, but finally, he slept.

When he awakened it was morning. There was a thread of light around one of the covers for the loopholes.

He dressed, and then opened one of the loopholes

153

and looked out. The sun was shining, and nothing was in sight. He took down the bar from the door and opened it . . . nothing.

The west wall of his shelter was of rock. The north side was within the cave itself, and a door there opened to allow access to the cave—not a big cave, but good for storage. And it was a stable for his horses, which could be brought in through a narrow passage alongside the east wall, where there was also a door.

The south wall faced outward, and blocked most of the cave entrance, but the roof of the cabin did not quite reach to the roof of the cave. There was a space of two or three feet, and he could climb out through a trap door to the roof. This gave access to a cleft in the rock that allowed an escape among stunted spruce on the mountainside out of sight of anyone near the cabin, or in front of it.

But though the place was secure, there was an enemy within that he had not made allowances for—his own imagination. One does not need enemies as long as the imagination can provide them.

Reuben Kelsey was not a man accustomed to being alone. It had been his way to surround himself with people who would cater to his whims or his vices, or those who were present merely to listen and admire. These people had been a cushion against the silence of solitude, which now he really knew for the first time.

He had taken the precaution of grazing his horses well before moving on to the hide-out, and later he had found a small glade hidden among the rocks with a thick carpet of grass. It was a natural corral where his horses could graze in the daylight hours.

On that first night, silence had come to him. Of course, it had been there through the long day, waiting in the wings. He had been conscious of it as he was conscious of the far-off sound of the wind among the pines, a distant sound that only intensified the stillness.

On this second day, after he had moved his horses to

154

the natural corral, he returned to the cabin and the silence closed in about him. Never given to reading, he had brought nothing along for that purpose. He cleaned his guns, checked his bridle and saddle, whittled, and felt the hours go by slowly. Finally he decided it must be getting on toward evening and stepped outside.

The sun was high in the sky ... it was scarcely noon. He went back inside and tried to sleep, but could not. Again he took the field glasses and climbed by the hidden trail to his vantage point.

There was no sound, no movement. The wind was chill off the mountains, but the sun was warm. He stayed there, high on the mountain, watching. Gradually, an eerie feeling came over him, for as he watched, he felt that eyes were watching him.

He slid down the mountain and returned to the hide-out.

Back there, he suddenly thought of Ten Brian, and again he wished his old companion had come with him. He had never thought much of any man or woman. He had found them, used them, tossed them aside, but his offer to Ten to join him had been sincere. Well ... up to a point.

In all his life Ten Brian had been the one person to whom his thoughts always returned. He had not stopped to ask himself why, but deep within him he began to realize for the first time that he had needed a friend. And he wished that friend had been Brian.

Even as a boy there had been something about Brian that rankled. Possibly it was the feeling that Brian could have bested him if he had tried ... no, it could not be that. Nobody had ever bested him in anything, and nobody would. But even as Brian irritated him, he had found he was the one person to whom he could talk. ... Why the hell hadn't he come along? What could he make out of the army business, after all? There was no future in that.

Then for a while he forgot Brian and thought of

155

what he would do with all that money when he got to
'Frisco. Invest some of it, of course. An investment
would provide a certain standing, and he'd be spoken
to with respect by men of affairs. But he would keep a
good bit for wine and for women.

Women . . .

Waiting wouldn't be so bad if he had a woman. Now
that Major's daughter . . . No wonder Ten was sweet on
her. In his mind he pictured her walking across the
parade ground as he had seen her once at the Fort. She
was somewhere in these hills right now. She might be
only a few miles away.

He paced the floor, looked outside. Then he climbed
back to his lookout again, scanned the rocks all around
to see from what places he might be observed. He
thought there were only two, and those difficult to
attain; he felt better.

The hills were green with young grass, the forest
fresh-looking and cool. Nothing moved. . . . There! He
moved the glasses, and after a moment found what he
was looking at . . . deer. Three of them, placidly feeding.

He scanned the hills. A lone eagle held still against
the sky. A rock rolled behind him and he jumped,
turning swiftly, gun in hand.

Irritated with himself, he went back to the cabin and
made coffee. He was breaking his rule against coffee in
the daytime, but there was nobody anywhere around,
and besides, he needed it.

He got a bottle of whiskey from his pack and a deck
of cards. He started to play solitaire, then gave up in
disgust. He leaned against the doorjamb and looked
out, but he saw nothing. He was alone.

Alone.

His original plan had been to remain here for three
weeks. Most of the war parties would have passed
southward by that time, the army would be gone, his
own men scattered.

156

Three weeks ... and on the second day he was irritable, uneasy, almost jumpy!

Reuben Kelsey was not really a drinker. He liked a drink and sometimes he took one, sometimes five or six, but sometimes he went weeks without touching the stuff and, generally speaking, he didn't care whether he did or not. Now, with nothing to do, he killed the bottle.

Somewhere along there he went to sleep, and awoke with sunlight showing through a crack at a loophole and a realization that time had passed. He started to sit up and his head swam. At last he got his feet on the floor and sat for some time with his head in his hands, his shock of hair falling forward.

After a long time he got up. The horses would need water. He had left them all night in their glade among the rocks.

Hitching up his pants, he tugged on his boots, with no recollection of taking them off the night before. He put on his gunbelt and took up his rifle, but his head was throbbing. He swore as he stepped to the door and opened it.

Instantly, he stopped. In the sand, not two feet from him, was a moccasin track.

He drew back, looking quickly around, but he saw nothing. He wet his lips.

They had found him, then. Had it been accident, or the coffee he made at the wrong time?

A beetle had crossed the track, so it had not been made within the past few minutes. Studying it, he decided it had been left sometime during the previous evening. He closed the door and went to the trap door and crawled out on the roof. With his glasses he studied the terrain before him, scanning the steep slope across the narrow valley, and looking down the valley at the wide sweep of country that opened below.

The sun was already high ... his *horses!*

Had the Indian found them? Hastily he slid from the

roof, and keeping under cover and wary of a trap, he scrambled over the rocks, and reached the glade where he had left the horses.

Gone!

For an instant he felt a wave of panic, then fury followed. Hastily he scrambled down to look at the tracks.

The story was plain enough. The Indian had followed the horse tracks to this place, had caught up the horses, and had led them out and down the trail. There he had tied them while he scouted around, probably going to the cabin then. Unable to get in, he had simply mounted up and ridden away, leading the stolen horses.

Reuben Kelsey knew that without a horse he was a dead man. Without the horses there was no possible escape, and no way he could pack out his gold.

He had to get away from here before that Indian came back with others, and somehow he had to find a horse.

His best bet was to go south toward South Pass and the settlement there, to keep under cover and steal a couple from the army if they were still there, or from some of his former men or whoever.

He went back into the cabin, closed the trap door carefully, and hid his gold in a hollow made under the corner of the wall. Then, taking food for several days, ammunition, and his rifle, he left the hide-out, crawled away through the rocks, in case the Indian was hidden somewhere watching, and started down the North Fork of the Popo Agie.

His head still throbbed, but his senses were keen and he knew well enough the danger he was in. Every step was a matter of life and death now.

Instinctively and from long practice he made his trail difficult if not impossible to follow. By nightfall he had covered what he guessed would be twelve miles.

He stopped then, ate some jerky and drank water, and rested a little. On the Middle Fork, with just enough light to see, he found no fresh tracks leading toward Sweetwater Gap. After another short rest he was up and moving.

Shortly after midnight, with no Indians to worry him at night time, he was on the Blue Ridge overlooking the silver gleam of Fiddler's Lake.

Kelsey slept the night there, burrowed into the needles and wrapped in his one blanket. Travel from here on would be increasingly dangerous, for here the war parties would go east or west, filtering down to the plains, and here there might be search parties of soldiers . . . with their horses.

At daybreak he was up, tired, but eager to be going. He worked his way down the slope, dogtrotted across a meadow and into the trees. Catching his breath there, he watched his back trail and saw nothing to worry him.

He cut across country toward the Little Popo Agie and found his first horse tracks just beyond it. They were a day old, but one of the horses was Ten Brian's big gray.

He found dry wood, and made coffee, ate jerky, and then killed his small fire, scattered the ashes, and sifted earth and leaves over the spot. If an Indian actually looked for it he would find it, but without a careful search he would see nothing amiss. Reuben Kelsey knew that, given time, a man could walk down a horse, and he knew that with the women to protect, Ten Brian would not be taking risks.

At a dogtrot he covered a couple of miles, then alternately walked and ran. By nightfall he was sure he had gained ground. The tracks looked fresh, and he had seen no Indians.

He slept the night through, but at the first hint of grayness in the sky he was up, chewing jerky and cutting for sign. He found it, and was off.

Running and walking, he kept to the trail of the horses. Shortly before noon, coming down a slope

159

through a clump of aspen to save time and cut off a wide bend in the trail, he saw them: horses feeding on the grass, saddles still in place, the big gray among them. They were close by, then. Ten Brian, somebody else, and the two women.

Reuben Kelsey eased himself down on his haunches and studied what lay before him. There was a fringe of trees along a trickle of water . . . no sign of a fire.

They were down there, and he could wait.

Chapter 20

The trickle of water Kelsey had seen came from a spring in a cluster of rocks. There were pines and aspens around the rocks, and a clump of low brush. The place offered excellent cover for a small party.

Jason and Brian took turns watching the horses grazing in the meadow. The horses as well as themselves needed the rest. Mary and Belle were asleep, worn out by the days of riding and hiding. Brian knew that in their state of exhaustion, he could no longer consider the ride to Fort Laramie. Regardless of the chances they might take, they must ride for South Pass.

The nooning, planned to last no more than an hour, stretched on as the women slept. Jason was in bad shape from his wounded arm, and Brian was fighting sleep, but soon he must awaken Jason to take over the watch.

The camp was a good one. There was even a place among the trees where the horses could be hidden after they had fed. Why not stay the night through and leave at daybreak?

South Pass could be no more than ten miles away, in a straight line, but by the trails they must follow it would be at least another five miles—too far for the women to ride in their present state, too far even for Jason. To rest through the day and night might be the

161

wisest plan and start fresh in the morning and go right on through without a stop.

He felt his eyes closing, and forced them open, then got to his feet, shaking his head to try to clear it. He moved around, keeping low and under cover of the trees.

Suddenly he noticed one of the horses—the one closest to the woods across the meadow. Its head was up, ears pricked.

Tenadore Brian took up his rifle and waited ... something or somebody was out there.

He let his eyes scan the edge of the trees opposite, then looked away, letting the peripheral vision pick up any movement, for sometimes a slight movement is seen better from the corners of the eyes. . . . There was no movement. Yet what was that shine from among the leaves?

He studied the area, looked all around, but saw nothing out of the usual. Yet he was sure there was something there. He eased down to his haunches, peering past the trunk of a pine, then he lowered one knee to the earth for a better shooting position.

Only the one horse had seemed nervous, but now Brian looked toward his gray. It was at the end of the picket rope but turned to face the trees, eating quietly but with the ears pricked. He knew from the past that the gray was alert and watching, even as it cropped grass.

Whoever waited out there had only to stay until they came for their horses, and he would be sure to get at least one of them. But would they wait?

Turning his head, Brian looked behind him at the place where the women and Jason lay asleep. None of them moved; all was still.

He looked again to the spot where he had seen that different shine, and as he looked a small rock or clump of dirt rolled from under the brush. Something back there had moved. He was tempted to shoot, but he had

162

never shot at any target he could not see or did not know was there. He had no desire to shoot an innocent person, or even an animal, so he held his fire.

Whoever it was would wait, as he had considered doing. They might remain where they were throughout the night. Yet soon the horses must be moved, and when dark came, they must be watered.

He studied the situation. The gray's picket stake was thirty-five or forty feet from the shelter of the trees. Mary's horse was no further away, but the other two were picketed out in the meadow a good sixty yards from shelter.

He could let Mary or Belle go for the horses, for there was small chance they would be fired on. Rather, it might lead the unknown watcher into a trap, as he might believe there was no man here with them. But the thought of exposing one of the women to even a slight chance of danger went against the grain. There had to be some other solution.

Another idea occurred to him. The horses out yonder had not whinnied as they would have done to another horse, and therefore the unknown in the trees across the meadow either had no horse or had left it some distance away. If he had no horse he would be wanting one desperately.

So what would happen? He—or they—would come during the night when a horse might be stolen with less risk. And it was at night that Brian himself must go after the horses.

He settled down to wait and to watch, and the horses, too, seemed to have settled down. Either the unknown in the trees had gone, or he had relaxed enough to make the horses less wary.

Slowly, time slipped away. It was warm and pleasant in the small grove. Jason moaned a little in his sleep, something he would never have done awake.

Several times Ten Brian caught himself dozing. He needed sleep, but not so bad as did the others. Despite

163

the rugged conditions, he had recovered somewhat. His headache was almost gone, and his lean, powerful body was asserting itself.

Finally he went down and awakened Mary. "Can you watch? I need some sleep before night."

She rose quickly, and leading her away from the others he explained the situation and advised her to watch the horses, and to be alert for any movement by the unknown watcher.

Taking his rifle, she moved up to where she could watch, and Brian lay down on the pine needles in a small hollow under a tree. He held his pistol in his hand.

It was dusk when she awakened him. "Ten, I thought something moved over there."

He got up quickly. The others were already awake. He had slept only about an hour, but even that small rest had refreshed him.

The horses were still at their picket ropes, but the gray was as close to the trees as it could get. Near a pile of rocks, several marmots were playing, evidence enough that nothing was moving over there.

"Mary," he whispered, "I'm going to try to get my gray horse. You cover me with the rifle. If anybody comes out from the trees over there . . . shoot."

He worked his way along the ridge, keeping under cover of the scattered trees and brush until he was close to the gray. He knew the horse would be expecting him, for it would be wanting water.

He spoke softly and the gray lifted its head and looked at him.

A bullet whapped against the rock within inches of his head and scattered him with stinging fragments. Almost with the same report, Mary fired.

The double report echoed, the sound drifted away, and all was still. Nothing moved except the horses, nervous at the firing. Mary, Brian decided, had fired at

164

the flash of the rifle over yonder, but it was unlikely she had hit anything.

But the shot had told him something. The man over there—and Brian was sure it was only one man—wanted a horse the worst way. At the first indication that someone might be approaching he had fired, risking everything to warn them away from the horses. It would be too dark to see in a matter of minutes, and he needed to know where the horses were, where their picket pins were located.

The trees and brush across the meadow were now a wall of blackness, and the area in between was vague and indistinct. If someone started to crawl toward the horses he would scarcely be able to see them . . . nor could anyone see him.

Brian went down the slight bank, and pistol in hand, wormed his way slowly across the grass. He crawled past the gray, pulled the picket pin, and then, whispering to the big horse, he swung to the saddle. Lying low along its neck he urged the horse toward those horses farthest out, keeping his gray at a slow walk, occasionally stopping it to simulate a horse cropping grass. He moved closer, caught another picket rope, and with a sharp tug, loosened the pin. Then he walked his horse on toward the next one. He was near it when suddenly a dark figure rose from the ground. He caught a glimpse of movement an instant before the man lunged, and he kicked the gray with his heel.

The horse leaped forward, and the attacker missed his lunge, but turned sharply as Brian did. In his hand there was a gleam from a knife blade.

"Is that you, Reub?" Brian asked.

"It is."

"Then get out of here while you've got a chance."

"I need a horse, boy—I need one bad. In fact, I need two horses."

"Get them from the Sioux. There's Indians all over the place."

"I'll take a couple of these," Kelsey replied easily. "I hate to do it, Ten." And then he added quietly, "I've got a gun on you, Ten. I can blast you out of the saddle."

"And I have one on you." It was Mary, speaking from the darkness. "I have you right against the sky."

Kelsey chuckled. "Now wouldn't you know it? It's always a woman who ruins a man. Ma'am, I think you're bluffin'. Show me you got a gun."

Mary was cool. "I have one all right."

"I have one too, Reub," Brian said, "laid right on you. It's an Army Colt, if you want to know, caliber .44, and I always could shoot, so you just back up.

"We haven't a horse for you, or I'd take you in a prisoner, and I'd take your gun, but I'd not want to leave any man afoot and unarmed in Indian country. You just back off, and figure yourself lucky.

"Mary, you get up on one of those horses. Gather the others and we'll start back."

Mary hesitated. "But you'll only have one gun on him, Ten. He might take a chance."

"Not if I know Kelsey. He likes a sure thing. Anyway, he can take his chance if he feels lucky."

Kelsey's chuckle was genuine. "You're right, Ten. I play the sure thing. You were a good shot, so I'll not chance it. We'll have to get together some other time. I'm holstering my gun, Ten, and backing off."

"You'll forgive me if I don't holster mine, I'm sure. Good-bye, Reub ... and good luck. You're going to need it."

His eyes were accustomed to the darkness now and he saw Reuben Kelsey slip his gun back into its holster.

"Ten, they tell me you been all over. Paris, Rome, China ... all them places. What're they like, Ten? I always figured someday I'd see them."

"They're worth seeing, Reub, really worth it. But don't try to talk me off guard. It won't work."

166

"It ain't that. I just wished I could have gone along. We should have stuck together, you and me."

Tenadore Brian believed that Kelsey was at least half sincere. He also knew the volatile nature of the man, who could change from sentiment to killing within a moment. He backed his horse away a few steps.

Was Kelsey really alone? There was no way of telling, and with Kelsey one must be ready for trickery at all times. Brian wanted to be away and riding . . . there could be no thought of spending the night here now. Somehow they would have to get away quickly.

Alert for any movement, he turned his horse slightly, still watching Kelsey.

"Ten, leave me a horse. I got to have one."

"We've just enough, Reub, so you'll have to get one from the Indians. So long, Reub."

He swung his horse in the opposite direction and rode a zigzag course toward the trees.

When he reached their shelter he looked back. He thought he could see Kelsey still standing there.

What would the man do? Without a horse, in that country, even a man like Kelsey was not going to last very long. And he could get nowhere with the gold, if he had it.

He could not even leave the mountains. As long as he remained here, in the Wind Rivers, he had water, he could rustle for food, and he could survive. But there was nowhere he could go from the mountains without a horse.

To go east into the Big Horns would simply put him in a worse situation, for the Sioux were there in numbers. West and south was open country, much of it without water, all of it exposed to view.

So what would he do? He would come after them, of course. He had no other choice.

He would follow them, steal a horse before they came to South Pass if that was possible; and if not, steal one at the settlement. He was not the kind of a

167

man to give up. He would have been a good man for this country if he had not chosen the wrong side of the law. But he had made his choice, and it led down a one-way road.

Jason was on his feet, but he looked bad. He was in no shape to ride, but there was no safety for them here. Their only chance was to make the settlement at South Pass and get whatever medical treatment the place would offer.

Mary was still in the saddle, Belle was gathering the few things scattered about.

"Ten, what do we do?" she asked.

He glanced at Mary. Her face was scarcely to be made out in the deeper darkness under the trees. "Ride," he said. "All we can do is ride."

Jason stood where a little light from the stars fell upon his face. "Can you make it, Jason?" Brian asked.

"I'll make it."

Belle mounted her horse and Ten Brian led the way. Hesitating at the edge of the clearing on the far side from where he had left Kelsey, he then rode quickly out, gun in hand.

He pointed to a square shoulder of rock against the sky. "Point for that. We'll pass a mite to the east of it."

They rode across the meadow at a fast gallop, then slowed where the way led up among the rocks.

Brian held back, letting Mary take the lead, for the danger would, he believed, come from behind. He saw the others go past, then waited a minute to listen for following hoof-beats, but none came. There was no sound but the wind. Turning, he followed the others.

Again he drew rein. He had an eerie sense of being watched, of being followed, but he knew his reactions were not normal ones, and it worried him. He listened, but heard no sound in the night.

Rock Creek should be not very far ahead. Beyond that they should come to Willow Creek and be able to follow it down to the settlement. But he had never followed Willow Creek, and had no idea what obstacles there might be. A blow-down in the forest, for instance, might force them to circle around it.

He caught up with the others, and they wove their uncertain way through the scattered forest. Occasionally he glimpsed the square shoulder of rock he used as a guide, but often it was out of sight, hidden behind trees. Once he almost dozed in the saddle, but was startled awake by a sudden cessation of movement. He saw all the horses bunched, and Mary had turned back to him.

"Ten, there's somebody or something up ahead. I don't know what it is."

He peered into the trees. Was it a fire he saw? A dying fire, perhaps? He listened, and heard no sound.

"I'll scout ahead," he whispered. "If there's any trouble, don't wait, don't think of me, just get out, fast."

He was wide awake now. How far had they come? Three or four miles? Scarcely that, for their course had been erratic with no regular trail to follow. He looked for the rock and saw it looming above, just a little ahead.

He took his rifle and went on, making no sound. He was wary, but his senses were dulled by weariness. The days of struggle, scarce food, and little sleep had taken their toll.

A voice came out of the darkness. "All right, sodger boy, you just stand. You just hold it right there where you are."

He stopped, swaying a little. He could not see the speaker, but his voice located him among the trees ahead, a dark patch that revealed nothing in the way of detail.

Behind him another voice spoke. "It's the women, Jess, and Jase with 'em!"

"Bring 'em in," Jess replied, "an' Jase, too. Do me good to see him again ... although it ain't going to do him much good."

169

Tenadore Brian swore softly. Trapped! With help only a few miles away, they had walked right into the hands of their enemies. He could see nothing at which to shoot, but he had an idea he himself was skylined, making him the perfect target.

Somebody else spoke up. "Throw some wood on the fire, an' let's see what we ketched."

Chapter 21

Ten Brian slumped in the saddle and suddenly through the fog of exhaustion there came an idea. Carefully he withdrew his feet from the stirrups. Brush was thick all about him with patches of grass between the clumps. As wood was thrown on the fire and it flared up, he let himself go and toppled from the saddle into the brush.

A shout went up, but he was already scrambling away among the brush. At least for the moment he was free."

"Jube! Get him! Get that damned lieutenant and kill him where you find him! Get him, man!"

Brian could hear a dozen men crashing into the brush. He had had no idea there were so many.

All of a sudden there was a shot, far away to the left, a shot and a gulping cry. There was silence.

The women and Jason still sat their horses. The renegades had suddenly disappeared. Somebody had been shot, and by an unknown . . . *who?*

For a long time there was stillness and then Jess spoke matter of factly. "There's only one of him, whoever he is. Bring the women in, boys, and dismount them. Whoever it is, we'll take him in and salt him down."

Brian fired at the sound of the voice, holding low

and shooting quickly, two shots, inches apart. Even as he triggered the last one he was rolling over swiftly, and came up to a crouch.

Fear had exploded his weariness. He was tense with excitement, not the best of moods to be in at the moment, but he was ready.

Several shots smashed into the brush where he had been.

"Good work, Ten!" The voice was forty or fifty yards off, by the sound of it . . . Reuben Kelsey's voice! "You an' me again. We can take 'em!"

"Kel!" somebody shouted. "What're you shootin' at us for? What's gone wrong?"

Kelsey's voice rumbled, a strange tone as though he were speaking against a rock wall and it was echoing back.

"Now, boys, you know I always liked a good fight, but I like to win, an' you boys are buckin' a stacked deck with Brian here. He ain't the kind to lose. An' those girls ain't for the likes of you. Me, maybe, but not you."

They were silent, and Brian could imagine what they were saying. They were caught in a cross fire if they moved, and although there were more of them—how many he had no idea—they were wondering if there were enough. He moved, crouching, through the brush, working nearer to them.

Jason still sat his horse, but Mary and Belle were on the ground. Both had taken their chance and slipped from their saddles. If Jason was even conscious it was remarkable. The silence continued. Nobody moved, each one waiting for some indication of what would happen next. Brian lay pressed against the earth . . . a bug crawled across his hand . . . he felt the breeze touch his cheek, ever so lightly.

The outlaws were not liking it very much, for they knew the kind of trouble Kelsey could bring them. At the same time they resented his interfering.

"Where's the gold, Reub? You got it with you?" one man asked presently.

Kelsey laughed . . . only that, but it seemed to enrage them. Half a dozen shots flashed, pointed toward the sound.

Kelsey laughed again.

Ten Brian, flat against the grass, inched his way along, working closer to where they waited. Where were Mary and Belle? They had dropped from their horses, but by now the renegades might have moved out to them. He paused to listen, then inched onward.

Where they came from he never knew, but suddenly several men lunged up from the brush and rushed at him. Rolling over on his back, he got off one shot with his rifle, then swung at the legs of the charging men.

He caught the nearest one across the shins and he screamed and fell forward, almost on top of Brian, who rolled over and came up fast, holding his rifle in both hands. He caught the nearest man with a butt stroke across the face, and then drove the barrel into the ribs of another.

The attackers closed in around him, but that was the sort of fighting he liked, and for which he had been trained. In the Foreign Legion they expect their enemies to close, and at close quarters there is no more effective weapon than a rifle butt in the hands of a man trained to use it.

As the first man lunged to get close, Brian delivered a short butt stroke that dropped him in his tracks Reversing the movement, he smashed the barrel into the stomach of the next man, then drove the butt against the chin of a third.

They had expected nothing like it, and had met no such attack before. Wild with fury and desperation, Brian waded in, smashing short blows to the head and body. Fearful of injuring each other, none of them fired.

He got his chance suddenly and squeezed off a shot

173

at a six-inch range. The man was driven back on his haunches, and a kick flattened him out. Suddenly the brutal fight was over.

One terrified man was scrambling away through the brush, another lay groaning on the grass. Two lay silent, merely dark shapes of what had been men.

He squatted quickly, fearful of being outlined against the sky, and crouched there, his breath tearing at his lungs in ragged gasps. He put the butt of his Henry against the ground and balanced himself with it, then went forward on his knees. The nearest man lay within arm's reach and Brian could see a faint gleam from his pistol butt. Reaching over, he drew the gun.

Mary was here, somewhere near him. Odd about that, he had known so many women, and beautiful women, but none he really wanted until he met Mary, and then all of a sudden he knew he had gone far enough. He knew how Major Devereaux felt and could not find it in himself to blame him. After all, he had come out of nowhere with no future that anybody could see, not even in the army, which would suffer from too many officers looking for places once the war was over.

There was Washington, perhaps. He had languages to help him, and knew more about the world's armies than most, but his kind of experience did not necessarily count for much. And the military mind is always slow to accept change.

Slowly his breathing returned to normal. . . . Where was Mary? And Belle? They had been close by, but he heard nothing, and he dare not make a sound that might give his position away. One bullet would be enough, and they would be desperate to kill him now.

Whatever was to happen had to happen soon. He felt he would cave in at any moment. He closed his eyes, and the lids felt hot and dry. There was no moisture on his lips . . . *fever?*

Somewhere a cricket was chirping, and a nighthawk

174

swooped low above him. He waited on his knees, no longer eager for a fight, just hoping they would go away and leave him.

But he must find Mary and Belle. They had been off to his left, he believed. He started to move, and heard a faint whisper.

"Ten?"

"Here!"

He kept his voice low, but not low enough, for there was the lash of a bullet through the leaves within inches of them. He flattened to the earth, and Mary did the same beside him. Her hand found his and they lay there while a rifle barked and half a dozen bullets scarched the area for them.

Suddenly, a man screamed, a wild, quivering scream of agony and fear . . . then silence.

For a long time then, they lay still, and there was no further sound, nor any movement near them. And somewhere along the line Tenadore Brian fell asleep.

A persistent tugging at his shoulder finally awoke him. "Ten! *Ten!* Wake up!"

Suddenly he was awake, awake in a blurred sort of way. He turned his head and peered around. He lay among low brush and stunted trees not thirty yards from the grove where the outlaws had sheltered themselves the night before.

Mary still tugged at him. "Ten! Please!"

"What—what is it?"

"It's almost light, Ten, and somebody is coming, over there." She pointed—not toward the grove.

It all came rushing back, and he looked around him. Two men lay dead upon the ground . . . another had crawled off somewhere.

Kelsey . . . Reuben Kelsey was coming, and he was in no shape to meet him.

He checked the spare pistol. The chambers were loaded, all six of them.

Belle was about fifteen yards away, and Jason was

on the ground beside her. Somehow he had gotten off his horse, or he had fallen off.

"Is he alive?" Brian asked.

"Yes, I think so. He was." She clung to his arm. Haggard as she was, her hair awry, her face dirty, she was still lovely.

"Ten, who is that out there?" Mary whispered.

"Kelsey."

"What about the others?"

"If he's coming after us, they're dead or gone. He might have slipped among them and killed them all . . . he could do it."

"What will we do?"

Brian looked at her. "I'll fight. I'll have to. If we try to leave, he'll shoot us down. If we give him an argument he'll smile and agree, and then he'll kill Jason and me at the first opportunity."

He stopped whispering to listen, and heard a chuckle close by. "Looks like you got it figured, boy. An' from the look of you you're in no shape for a fight."

Kelsey stood there, a gun in his hand. Brian's gun held steady on him, and Kelsey smiled.

"Never thought it would end like this, did you, boy?"

"Oddly enough, I did," Brian replied honestly. "I always knew it would come to a showdown between us someday."

Kelsey chuckled again. "You want it with guns? If we shoot from here neither of us is going to get out alive."

"I had that in mind. I'd go cheerfully to take you with me right now."

"Yeah? Well, I wouldn't. You want it with knives? I want to warn you I'm almighty good with one. Hear that man scream last night? I had to convince those boys that they'd better run whilst they could, so I gave it a little twist where he'd feel it most."

"You choose . . . knives or fists, I don't care."

Kelsey looked over at Mary. "He's got nerve, that one. Real nerve. Nobody would ever face me with a knife."

Brian shrugged. "A knife is a stupid weapon in most hands," he said. "You'd be asking for trouble, you know. I spent too much time around the world not to know about knives."

His gun muzzle wavered not at all. Even as he talked he knew that Kelsey might elect to shoot at any instant, and he must be ready. He would know when Kelsey was going to shoot, and Kelsey would know if he started to, and at that range neither was going to miss.

He was on the ground, one knee pressed against the grass. Kelsey, on his feet, had the advantage.

The sleep had done him good, and he knew he would need every bit of intelligence and strength he possessed. This was the showdown.

Kelsey needed a horse ... at least two horses if he was to escape with the gold. He also wanted the girls, and he did not want a witness. If he could escape from here, go to the west coast and change his name, he would be believed dead, and would be free to enjoy the gold.

His word and the fact they had long known each other meant nothing at all. He had turned on his own men, robbed them, deserted them, and killed some of them.

"You said you wanted a horse, Reub. There should be some horses left over yonder when your boys took out. You just get on a horse and ride away."

"Tried it that way. I holed up in a place I had, but I ain't one for bein' alone, Ten. I like folks about me, so I just figure I'll take the horses you've got and both of these womenfolks. They'll keep me company until I decide to ride on."

Both of them were playing for time. Brian knew it had to break any instant, only one move ...

Belle was the one who did it. She knew Brian needed

177

a break, and she threw a small stone at the nearest horse. The stone struck it on the hip and the horse side-stepped suddenly. Kelsey moved like a cat.

He turned sharply toward the sound, dropping into a half crouch . . . a fact that caused Brian's shot to miss.

Brian snapped off his shot, then left the ground in a lunge. Kelsey wheeled, fired, and missed, and the two men rushed together.

Brian's hard left fist smashed Kelsey over the eye as they came together. Kelsey's shot missed, the bullet tearing Brian's shirt. Striking down at the gun with his own gun barrel, he knocked it from Kelsey's hand.

Instantly he started to step back to order Kelsey to lift his hands, but the big outlaw was having none of it. He never stopped moving, for as the gun was knocked from his hand he threw an arm over Brian's gun arm and locked it under his armpit in a grip of iron. Brian slugged him in the wind and they battled fiercely, each with one hand free.

A branch tore the gun from Brian's hand and he ducked his head and butted Kelsey in the face, driving his boot-heel down on his instep at the same instant.

Kelsey jerked free, landed a right to the face that shook Brian to his heels, and then they stood toe to toe and battered each other with driving fists, moving back and forth over the small grassy space where they had come together.

Brian broke loose, feinted, and when Kelsey came in, met his rush with a right to the wind. Kelsey brought up short, clubbed a left to Brian's head that cut him over the eye, then bored in, slamming wicked punches at the body.

They clinched, and Brian resisted fiercely, then suddenly yielded and went over backwards by intention, throwing Kelsey on over his head. Both men came up fast, but Brian, having planned the move, was up first. As Kelsey came off the ground Brian broke his nose

178

with a right to the face, then slammed a left to the ribs as Kelsey came in.

For a moment they clung together, gasping for breath. Desperate, Brian knew he must win, and he must win quickly. He had no stamina now for a long fight, and Kelsey was the stronger and bigger man.

Brian pulled back, smashed an elbow to Kelsey's face, over and back. But the man had a neck like a bull, and the elbow seemed to have little effect.

They broke loose, exchanged punches, then clinched again. Kelsey wrapped his powerful arms around him and tried to force him over backwards. Brian stabbed his thumbs into Kelsey's groin, and as the bigger man drew back his hips to escape them, Brian slipped an arm around Kelsey's waist, then grabbed Kelsey's right sleeve and threw him over his hip to the ground.

Reuben Kelsey hit the ground hard, and started to get up. A right swing to the face knocked him sprawling. He rolled over and tried to dive for Brian's legs, but Ten stepped back.

Kelsey started to rise, then dived sidewise for a gun that lay where it had fallen when the fight began. His fingers closed over it and he rolled over to fire.

Ten Brian's hand dropped to his own gun. He drew and fired in one movement. The bullet caught Kelsey in the chest, slamming him back against the ground. He started to rise again, feeling for the gun he had dropped, but his eyes were on Brian.

"It ain't goin' to work," he said. "Nobody can kill Reuben Kelsey, I—"

Tenadore Brian waited, gun in his fist, not wanting to shoot again.

"Somebody is coming," Mary said, "I think they are soldiers."

Reuben Kelsey lay back, his breath coming in hoarse gasps. There was a froth of blood on his lips. His face was fearfully battered from Brian's punches. He rolled over, got his knees under him, and tried to rise. "Got a

179

lot o' gold," he muttered. "No place to wait without a woman. A man needs a—"

He got all the way to his feet, but without his gun.

"Brian, I always liked you," he said, "but I always knew I could take you. I figured we'd have it to do sooner or later, you an' me."

He spoke coolly, and only a little blood showed at his lips. His shirt was soaking with it.

"I'd of had this country whupped if you hadn't come back."

"You didn't have a chance, Reub, not with me here or without me. Major Devereaux would have had you sooner or later."

"Anyway . . . anyway I run that bunch off. Pack o' yellow . . . yellow . . ."

His knees gave way under him and he fell. "Anyway," he said, "I got the gold, I got—"

"You've got nothing." It was Cahill. "We came over Jackass Pass and found your cabin. Turpenning spotted a few crumbs of fresh dirt and located your cache. We've got the gold now."

Reuben Kelsey lay still, breathing hoarsely. "Huh . . . missed out, missed all around." He opened his eyes. "Ten, we started together. What . . . what happened?"

"The road forked, Reub. The road forked, and you took the wrong turn."

Cahill swung down. "I'm no doctor, but I can help. I'll just have a look." He knelt beside the outlaw, and then he looked up. "Ten, this man is dead."

He bent over Kelsey's body, trying for some sign of life. There was none. Cahill got to his feet.

"Lieutenant," he said regretfully, "I hope you will understand this, but my orders are to place you under arrest."

"I do understand. Shall we start back?"

Brian climbed into the saddle, his weariness closing

180

over him like a fog. "How about Ironhide? Did he come back to camp?"

"Yes. He's safe." Then Cahill added, "I might say that he made a statement that clarified matters considerably and is much in your favor."

Mary rode up beside him as they started away. "What will happen, Ten?"

"There will be a hearing to see if I warrant a court-martial. I doubt if your father or Colonel Collins will insist. There should be an investigation. I was absent without leave, I ordered the pay wagon and your escort away from the wagon train on my own initiative. Those are serious matters."

"Pa always said what the Army needed most was officers who were not afraid to act."

Brian smiled. "Exactly. And if everything turns out right they may be commended, may even become heroes. If it turns out wrong, they can be court-martialed."

"It doesn't matter," Mary said quietly. "I want to be with you, whatever happens."

Cahill drew up on the brow of a hill to wait for the burial party to catch up. Brian looked off across the vast sweep of country past the Beaver Rim and southward toward the Honeycomb Buttes and the Red Desert.

This was a country. No wonder the Indians were prepared to fight for it.

Tenadore Brian waited nervously in the dusty street of South Pass City. Cahill had made his report, and the gold had been placed in the Major's care. The Major had talked to his daughter and to Belle Renick. For the first time they learned the details of the massacre of the wagon train.

Cahill emerged from the door of the hotel and jerked a thumb over his shoulder. "The Major will see you now, Ten. Luck."

"I'll need it," Brian replied, and went in.

Major Devereaux looked at him critically. Lieutenant Brian's uniform, much the worse for wear, had been carefully brushed and cleaned. Despite its condition he looked what he was, a dashing hell-for-leather cavalry officer of the kind the service needed.

"Lieutenant, I will want your report in detail, a written report, to forward to the commanding officer." He got to his feet and thrust out his hand. "In the meantime, Lieutenant, let me say that you did a remarkable job under difficult circumstances. That will be all."

"All?"

"Yes. Oh, by the way, Mary suggested I ask you for dinner tonight. Could you manage it?"

"With pleasure, sir."

Lieutenant Tenadore Brian stepped back, saluted, did a sharp right face, and walked out of the door.

Major Devereaux looked after him and sighed. Well, Mary could do a lot worse, a whole lot worse.

Damn it, the man was a *soldier*.

ABOUT THE AUTHOR

LOUIS L'AMOUR, born Louis Dearborn L'Amour, is of French-Irish descent. Although Mr. L'Amour claims his writing began as a "spur-of-the-moment thing," prompted by friends who relished his verbal tales of the West, he comes by his talent honestly. A frontiersman by heritage (his grandfather was scalped by the Sioux), and a universal man by experience, Louis L'Amour lives the life of his fictional heroes. Since leaving his native Jamestown, North Dakota, at the age of fifteen, he's been a longshoreman, lumberjack, elephant handler, hay shocker, flume builder, fruit picker, and an officer on tank destroyers during World War II. And he's written four hundred short stories and over fifty books (including a volume of poetry).

Mr. L'Amour has lectured widely, traveled the West thoroughly, studied archaeology, compiled biographies of over one thousand Western gunfighters, and read prodigiously (his library holds more than two thousand volumes). And he's watched thirty-one of his westerns as movies. He's circled the world on a freighter, mined in the West, sailed a dhow on the Red Sea, been shipwrecked in the West Indies, stranded in the Mojave Desert. He's won fifty-one of fifty-nine fights as a professional boxer and pinch-hit for Dorothy Kilgallen when she was on vacation from her column. Since 1816, thirty-three members of his family have been writers. And, he says, "I could sit in the middle of Sunset Boulevard and write with my typewriter on my knees; temperamental I am not."

Mr. L'Amour is re-creating an 1865 Western town, christened Shalako, where the borders of Utah, Arizona, New Mexico, and Colorado meet. Historically authentic from whistle to well, it will be a live, operating town, as well as a movie location and tourist attraction.

Mr. L'Amour now lives in Los Angeles with his wife Kathy, who helps with the enormous amount of research he does for his books. Soon, Mr. L'Amour hopes, the children (Beau and Angelique) will be helping too.

BANTAM'S #1
ALL-TIME BESTSELLING AUTHOR
AMERICA'S FAVORITE WESTERN WRITER

- ☐ THE LONELY MEN   11076 • $1.50
- ☐ CATLOW   10986 • $1.50
- ☐ LANDO   10837 • $1.50
- ☐ KIOWA TRAIL   10831 • $1.50
- ☐ THE BURNING HILLS   10829 • $1.50
- ☐ THE MAN FROM THE BROKEN HILLS 10827 • $1.50
- ☐ KILRONE   10799 • $1.50
- ☐ GALLOWAY   10795 • $1.50
- ☐ CALLAGHEN   10768 • $1.50
- ☐ THE QUICK AND THE DEAD   10761 • $1.50
- ☐ OVER ON THE DRY SIDE   10742 • $1.50
- ☐ DOWN THE LONG HILLS   10691 • $1.50
- ☐ THE DAY BREAKERS   10687 • $1.50
- ☐ WESTWARD THE TIDE   10491 • $1.50
- ☐ KID RODELO   10449 • $1.50
- ☐ BROKEN GUN   10446 • $1.50
- ☐ WHERE THE LONG GRASS BLOWS 10286 • $1.50
- ☐ HOW THE WEST WAS WON   2478 • $1.50

Buy them at your local bookstore or use this
handy coupon for ordering:

Bantam Books, Inc., Dept. LL, 414 East Golf Road, Des Plaines, Ill. 60016

Please send me the books I have checked above. I am enclosing $_____
(please add 50¢ to cover postage and handling). Send check or money order
—no cash or C.O.D.'s please.

Mr/Mrs/Miss_____

Address_____

City_____State/Zip_____

LL2—8/77

Please allow four weeks for delivery. This offer expires 8/78.